What on earth was he doing?

Matt knew you didn't fool around with your best friend's sister unless you were plenty serious about her. And Matt had no intention of getting serious about any woman.

He abruptly pulled back from their passionate kiss. "Sorry," he muttered. "I don't know what happened."

"Weddings make people sentimental," Ali mumbled.

"That must be it."

Ali's fingers drifted to her lips, where the imprint of Matt's mouth still burned. His kiss had affected her like nothing in her experience, sending her senses spinning until she was dazed and confused. How could a simple thing like a kiss make her feel as if the world had suddenly careened off its axis?

She wasn't looking for romance with a man like Matt. She would just have to forget how he'd forever changed her perception of what a kiss could be.

Yeah, right.

Dear Reader,

What makes a man a Fabulous Father? For me, he's the man who married my single mother when she had three little kids (who all needed braces) and raised us as his own. And, to celebrate an upcoming anniversary of the Romance line's FABULOUS FATHERS series, I'd like to know *your* thoughts on what makes a man a Fabulous Father. Send me a brief (50 words) note with your name, city and state, giving me permission to publish all or portions of your note, and you just might see it printed on a special page.

Blessed with a baby—and a second chance at marriage—this month's FABULOUS FATHER also has to become a fabulous husband to his estranged wife in *Introducing Daddy* by Alaina Hawthorne.

"Will you marry me, in name only?" That's a woman's desperate question to the last of THE BEST MEN, Karen Rose Smith's miniseries, in *A Groom and a Promise*.

He drops her like a hot potato, then comes back with babies and wants her to be his nanny! Or so he says...in *Babies and a Blue-Eyed Man* by Myrna Mackenzie.

When a man has no memory and a woman needs an instant husband, she tells him a little white lie and presto! in *My Favorite Husband* by Sally Carleen.

She's a waitress who needs etiquette lessons in becoming a lady; he's a millionaire who likes her just the way she is in *Wife in Training* by Susan Meier.

Finally, Robin Wells is one of Silhouette's WOMEN TO WATCH—a new author debuting in the Romance line with *The Wedding Kiss*.

I hope you enjoy all our books this month—and every month!

Regards,

Melissa Senate,
Senior Editor

Please address questions and book requests to:
Silhouette Reader Service
U.S.: 3010 Walden Ave., P.O. Box 1325, Buffalo, NY 14269
Canadian: P.O. Box 609, Fort Erie, Ont. L2A 5X3

THE WEDDING KISS

Robin Wells

Silhouette®
ROMANCE™
Published by Silhouette Books
America's Publisher of Contemporary Romance

To Ken, my real-life romantic hero, and my parents,
Charlie Lou and Roscoe Rouse, who raised
me amid the magic of books.
Special thanks to Susan, Bob, Laura and Linda for the
coffeehouse critiques and encouragement.

 SILHOUETTE BOOKS

ISBN 0-373-19185-5

THE WEDDING KISS

Copyright © 1996 by Robin Rouse Wells

Printed in U.S.A.

ROBIN WELLS

Before becoming a full-time writer, Robin was a public relations executive whose career ran the gamut from writing and producing award-winning videos to organizing pie-throwing classes taught by circus clowns. At other times in her life she has been a model, a reporter and even a charm school teacher. But her lifelong dream was to become an author, a dream no doubt inspired by having parents who were both librarians and who passed on their own love of books.

Robin lives just outside New Orleans with her husband and two young daughters, Taylor and Arden. Although New Orleans is known as America's Most Romantic City, Robin says her personal romantic inspiration is her husband, Ken.

Robin is an active member of the Southern Louisiana chapter of the Romance Writers of America. She won the national association's 1995 Golden Heart award for best short contemporary novel and was a finalist in the 1994 "Heart of the Rockies" RWA contest.

When she's not writing, Robin enjoys gardening, antiquing, discovering new restaurants and spending time with her family.

Dear Reader,

Have you ever wanted to do something so badly you were afraid to give it a try?

Well, that's how I felt about writing a novel. Ever since I first learned to read and write, I've been scribbling down stories and telling myself that someday I'd write a book. It was such a closely held dream I was afraid to actually put it to the test.

When I gave birth to my first child four years ago, I began to realize how easily "somedays" could turn into "nevers." Time seemed to accelerate to warp speed as that little baby grew and changed right before my eyes. As I thought about her future, it occurred to me that one of the things I most wanted to give her was the confidence to pursue her dreams. Whatever she wanted to do or be, I hoped she'd have the courage to *go* for it.

One of the best ways I could help her was by setting a good example. It was time to write that book!

I joined the local chapter of Romance Writers of America, became active in a critique group and took a course called "Writing the Romance Novel." But most important, I wrote. And wrote. And wrote!

My first manuscript didn't sell and, looking at it now, I can see why. I had a lot to learn.

You can imagine how thrilled I was when Silhouette Associate Editor Cristine Niessner called to say she wanted to buy my second effort, *The Wedding Kiss*. When it won RWA's national Golden Heart competition, I was elated. When Cristine told me I was going to be Silhouette Romance's WOMEN TO WATCH author for 1996, I was walking on air. And when she bought two more of my novels less than seven months after the first, I needed to be peeled off the ceiling!

I hope you enjoy reading this book as much as I enjoyed writing it. And whatever your own dreams are, I hope you chase them till you catch them.

Sincerely,

Robin Wells

Chapter One

Matt Jordan threw open the pink door of the True Love Bridal Salon with such force that the beribboned bouquet of dried flowers attached to the door knocker fell to the floor. Scowling, he bent and retrieved the brittle bouquet from the pink carpet, only to have several flowers disintegrate in his hand. He was beginning to feel like a bull in a china shop, and the fact did nothing to improve his mood.

"May I help you?" A thin, blue-haired lady scurried toward him, looking as dry and withered as the blossoms.

"I'm here to see Ali McAlester."

The woman eyed the crumpled bouquet and closed the door behind him with exaggerated care. She was a good foot shorter than Matt, yet she somehow managed to look down her nose at him. "I'm afraid Miss McAlester can't be disturbed," she said in an imperious tone. "She's involved in the final fitting of her gown."

Final fitting! So what he'd overheard at the lumberyard was true—Ali *was* going to walk down the aisle with Derrick Atchison.

Over my dead body, Matt thought grimly. *I owe Robert that much.*

"I don't care if she's in the final fitting of her birthday suit," Matt said tersely. "I need to see her, and I need to see her *now.*"

The woman placed her hands on her scrawny hips and peered at him over the top of her pince-nez. "Are you the groom?" she inquired. "We don't allow our grooms to see any of our dresses before the ceremony. It's bad luck, you know."

If the situation weren't so serious, he might have been amused. He'd tried marriage once and had no intention of ever getting roped into that racket again. "You can rest assured that I'm not the groom."

"Then whom shall I say is calling?"

Oh, for Pete's sake—did he look like he was here to pay a social call? Matt was anxious to get this over with, and he was fast losing patience with this pretentious old biddy.

"Matt Jordan."

"Why don't you have a seat, Mr. Jordan, and I'll see if Miss McAlester can receive you." The woman waved a haughty hand toward a spindly-legged gilt chair that scarcely looked sturdy enough to stand up under its own weight, much less his six-foot-two frame.

Matt watched her sweep through a lace-draped doorway at the back of the shop and considered following her into the inner sanctum. The prospect of encountering a gaggle of dizzy, half-dressed brides was the only thing that held him in check.

Mumbling an oath, Matt turned and paced the tiny shop. He felt distinctly out of place in this bastion of femininity. The fact that the room was cloyingly pink, heavily perfumed and filled with reams of lace and gauze and other frilly doodads did nothing to put him at ease.

No question about it; he was completely out of his element, and it wasn't just a matter of his surroundings. *This is what you get for having a business partner,* he thought glumly. *If you hadn't merged your home building company with Robert's architectural firm, you wouldn't be involved in his family's personal problems.*

Not that their company hadn't been profitable. It had—and their latest project was sure to be the most successful ever.

No, the problem wasn't the partnership, he admitted to himself; the problem was a lack of planning—the very thing he prided himself on. Matt was a firm believer that good, sound planning was the basis of a successful life, and he considered his ability to look ahead and anticipate problems to be his chief talent.

So why the heck hadn't he planned what would happen to the company if one of them died? It was an oversight, pure and simple. He should have planned for any eventuality. Still, how was he supposed to know that Robert was going to get killed in a car crash and leave his share of the company to his ditzy sister?

Matt sighed deeply at the thought. Robert had not only been his business partner, he'd been his best friend since college, and Matt missed him something fierce. Their friendship was the reason Matt felt obligated to look after his sister. And from what Robert had told him, Ali needed plenty of looking after.

Matt had only met her once, but Robert had told him all the Ali stories. He knew how Robert had gotten arrested for indecent exposure while changing clothes in his car—all because Ali had sewn a tuxedo for him and he hadn't had the heart to let her know he wasn't going to wear the homemade monstrosity to a formal dance. And he'd heard about the time she'd mailed her brother a coconut cream pie—and given him a near-lethal dose of ptomaine poisoning. Then there was the time she'd advertised for a roommate when she moved to Dallas—and ended up sharing her apartment with a woman who was so convinced she was the reincarnation of Cleopatra that she'd tried to build a barge in the living room.

Everything the woman did resulted in chaos, and Matt was glad she lived a good five-hour drive away. He liked his life just the way it was—calm, well-ordered and predictable. The fewer dealings he had with Ali, the better. So far, he hadn't had to deal with her at all since her attorney was handling the settlement of Robert's estate.

Not that Ali needed representation where he was concerned; he fully intended to split the company's assets right down the middle. Ali would get Robert's fair share of the profits as soon as they sold the homes in the development that was now under construction, and afterward he'd be free to carry on as an independent businessman.

His desire to stay well clear of Little-Miss-Disaster-Looking-For-a-Place-To-Happen had been overridden by his sense of responsibility, however, when he'd overheard Hank Townsend's phone conversation at the lumberyard this morning. He'd distinctly heard Hank say that Ali McAlester was going to walk down the aisle with Derrick and that she was already back in Hillsboro, getting outfitted at the town's only bridal salon.

Matt had headed directly to the bridal shop. He owed it to Robert to prevent his sister from marrying a sleazeball with a well-known reputation for gambling and womanizing. Derrick had no doubt launched a long-distance romance with Ali just to get his hands on her inheritance, Matt thought grimly. The idea of that piece of scum taking advantage of Robert's sister and spending Robert's hard-earned money made Matt's blood boil.

Just thinking about it again caused Matt to lengthen his stride until he was crossing the room in only five steps. He was determined to talk some sense into the dizzy dame if it was the last thing he did.

What the heck was taking her so long anyway?

Looking for a distraction, he stopped in front of a display case and studied the items inside. What the devil were those frilly things? They looked like giant, lace-covered rubberbands. After staring at them a moment, he realized he was gawking at a set of garters.

Muttering an expletive, he turned toward the window and tried to see the street through the overcrowded display of mannequins.

"Hello, Matt."

It was about time! Matt whipped around, ready to give Ali a piece of his mind.

But the sight that greeted him stopped him short. She was enveloped in a cloud of pink, and it looked like she was floating.

Matt blinked. No, it was just the way her gown billowed out when she moved. He blinked again, then swallowed hard. Jiminy! She didn't look anything like the grief-stricken, weeping waif he'd met at Robert's funeral six months ago.

She looked....gorgeous. With everything Robert had told him about her, how had he managed to leave out that fact?

Stop staring, Jordan. Matt directed his gaze to a spot over her shoulder and tried to collect his thoughts.

Okay, so she was a knockout. It didn't change the fact that she could give lessons to Calamity Jane—or the fact that she was about to marry the town bum. Who'd ever heard of a pink wedding gown, anyway? Come to think of it, though, who'd ever heard of Ali McAlester doing *anything* in a normal fashion?

"I appreciate the thought, but I plan to carry flowers just a tad bit fresher than those," she said with a teasing note in her voice.

Matt followed her gaze down to the ridiculously battered bouquet still in his hand, which by now was little more than a batch of dried stems tied with pink and white ribbons.

Ali laughed, and Matt looked up to find himself the focus of a smile so bright it could have caused a power outage. Or power surge, Matt thought as a jolt of attraction raced through him. His eyes traveled the length of her, taking in the way the dress clung to her slender waist and revealed a delectable glimpse of cleavage. Her dark chestnut hair was swept up in some sort of tousled arrangement, her eyes were the color of a stormy sky and her complexion somehow reminded him of magnolia petals. He had a sudden urge to touch her cheek to see if it felt as soft and velvety as it looked.

Disconcerted, Matt rubbed his jaw. He hadn't thought about her in these terms before.

Thought about her in *what* terms? His train of thought must have completely derailed, Matt told himself irritably. Ali wasn't a—a—*woman.* Well, she obviously was, but not like *that*—at least, not as far as he was concerned. Not a woman with a capital *W*.

More like trouble with a capital T. Matt gave himself a mental shake. Ali was a nuisance, that was all, and he was here to keep her from making another of her infamous mistakes. Instead of standing here ogling her décolletage, he needed to be figuring out a way to tell her she was engaged to a total cad.

"We need to talk," he said in a voice that came out harsher than he intended. "Change into something more sensible and meet me at the coffee shop on the corner."

Her brow knit into a worried frown. "Is something wrong?"

Oh, something was wrong, all right. Several things, in fact. For starters, he wasn't supposed to be having these lascivious thoughts about his late partner's sister. And he hated the fact he had to tell her the truth about her fiancé. It was sure to be an emotional scene, and he made a point of avoiding those almost as much as he avoided matrimony.

But his biggest immediate problem was that he was too darn distracted by the way she looked in that dress to even think straight.

For the umpteenth time since the accident, he wished Robert were here. "You and I have some business to discuss," he evaded.

Ali studied his face for a moment. He was relieved when she nodded without asking any further questions. "I'll meet you in ten minutes."

Matt watched her shapely pink back disappear into the rear of the shop, then tossed the bouquet on a counter and strode out the door. Outside, he drew a deep breath of fresh air and headed down Main Street to the Cattlemen's Café. The cold March air felt good on his face. He'd gotten overheated in the shop—and the way Ali had looked in that dress hadn't helped in the least.

Ali wriggled out of the organza gown and distractedly handed it to the elderly saleswoman who'd insisted on accompanying her into the cramped dressing room. She was too absorbed in her thoughts of Matt Jordan to pay much attention to the woman's rambling chatter.

Ali hadn't remembered that Matt was so tall—or so good-looking. Of course, she'd only met him once before, and that had been at Robert's funeral. She hadn't been in any shape to notice anyone or anything then.

Matt had positively discombobulated her today, standing there with that ragged bouquet in his hand, his dark eyes raking her body. Her skin had warmed under his gaze and her heart had started racing. Her pulse still hadn't returned to normal.

"I'll adjust the hem and have your gown ready by tomorrow afternoon," the saleslady was saying.

Her words jarred Ali out of her reverie. "Thank you. That'll be fine," she replied. "Is Susan's dress finished yet?"

The woman nodded. "She came by for it this morning."

Ali smiled at the thought of her oldest and dearest friend. "How does she look in it?"

An expression that could have been a smile added more wrinkles to the saleslady's crinkled face. "Beautiful. Miss Connors will make a lovely bride, and you will make a lovely maid of honor." The woman swept out of the cubicle bearing Ali's dress as if it were a precious artifact.

Ali pulled on her sweater, a vague wistfulness overtaking her. She was delighted that Susan was getting married, but there was something about her best friend's impending wedding that stirred up all kinds of thoughts and feelings and longings. It made Ali think about things like home and family and roots—things that made up a successful life, things that weren't measured in dollars or business titles.

Ali hadn't made a lot of time for those things in the last few years and her brother's death six months ago had made her keenly regret it. Susan's wedding had brought it all into focus. As her friend's wedding plans had progressed, so had a vague idea Ali had harbored since Robert's funeral.

It was a great idea, one that would allow her to fulfill a personal goal as well as a professional one. Besides, it made perfect sense. All that remained was to convince Matt.

Matt. Ali's heart rate soared again at the thought of him.

Judging from the way he'd scowled at her, she might have her work cut out for her there. All she knew about him was what she'd heard from her brother. "We think exactly alike," Robert had said. That could only mean one thing: she was dealing with a hard-nosed pragmatist.

It also meant Matt undoubtedly shared her brother's view of her as an impractical scatterbrain. Robert had loved to regale his friends with tales of her mishaps and Matt was sure to have heard the gory details of every single one. It wouldn't be easy convincing him she was capable and competent.

Thinking about being competent made Ali glance at her watch, then hurriedly scramble into her slacks. Robert had said Matt was a stickler for punctuality and she didn't want to keep him waiting.

Matt was swallowing a gulp of coffee when Ali pushed open the glass door of the Cattleman's Café, jangling the cowbells overhead. He set the green mug down hard on the Formica tabletop and watched her scan the room. Draped in a black wool cape with a vivid red lining and toting a large black bag, she looked like a sexy version of Little Red Riding Hood. She pushed back the hood, ruffling her hair, and Matt felt a surge of attraction.

Quit ogling her like the Big Bad Wolf, he reprimanded himself.

Ali spotted him and quickly made her way to the table, flashing him a friendly grin as she slid onto the booth seat across from him. "Hi. What's up?"

Matt eyed her uncertainly. While he'd been waiting for her, he'd mentally run through half a dozen ways to broach the subject. None of them made the topic more palatable. Might as well go with his usual straightforward approach, he decided. "We have a serious situation we need to discuss," he began.

Ali smiled companionably. "It must be quite a situation to bring you to the bridal salon looking for me. How did you know where I was?"

"I, uh, overheard Hank Townsend mention it."

Her grin widened. "I didn't know you knew Hank. Are you coming to the wedding?"

The question caught Matt by surprise. Weren't guests supposed to receive written invitations to weddings? From what he'd heard about how Ali usually operated, though, he wouldn't be surprised if she'd invited guests telepathically.

"I'm not sure," he hedged. "When is it?"

"This Saturday," she replied.

Saturday! Derrick wasn't wasting any time. Matt decided he'd better not beat around the bush, either.

He placed his elbows on the table and leaned forward. "Let me get right to the point. How well do you know Derrick Atchison, Ali?" he asked.

She shrugged her shoulders. "Fairly well, I guess. I went to high school with him."

"Have you seen much of him since then?"

"Well, no." Ali paused to order an ice tea from the waitress. "I hadn't seen Derrick since graduation until I ran into him at a party last weekend."

Matt stared at her incredulously. "You hadn't seen him in years until last weekend? That must have been some reunion." He couldn't keep an edge of irony out of his voice. "Yessir, I'd say you two must have really hit it off."

Ali shot him a quizzical look. "What's this all about, Matt?"

Matt set down his coffee so hard that it threatened to slosh out of the cup. "Look, Ali, I know this is none of my business—but how can you walk down the aisle with someone you barely know?"

Ali regarded him strangely. "It's no big deal, Matt. People do it all the time."

She's even goofier than I thought. Matt ran a hand down his face and decided to drop the questions. "I have a few things to tell you about Derrick that might make you change your mind."

"I doubt there's anything you can tell me about him that I haven't already heard," she said with a serene smile. "Hillsboro is a pretty small town, and I've stayed in touch with my old friends here.''

Matt felt his mouth fall open. He closed it with an effort and rubbed his jaw. She was the most illogical female he'd ever encountered. *Try another approach,* he told himself, but he had no idea what might work with a person as completely devoid of common sense as Ali seemed to be.

The waitress delivered Ali's tea, and Matt watched her squeeze a lemon slice into the glass as he considered his next move. Maybe if he could figure out why she was marrying Derrick, he could figure out a way to stop her.

He forced what he hoped was a composed expression onto his face, deliberately trying to keep his voice low and controlled. ''Why are you doing this, Ali?''

Her eyebrows lifted in surprise. ''Because I was asked,'' she replied in an overly patient tone, the kind one might use when explaining something obvious to a halfwit. ''It's an honor, and I believe it's the kind of thing a person should do for an old friend if there's any way she possibly can.''

Matt couldn't have been more stunned if she'd announced she planned to dance naked on the church steeple. ''Of all the absurd, inane, ridiculous things I've ever heard...'' He shook his head in disbelief. ''When Robert told me you were unpredictable, I didn't know he meant you were flat-out crazy.''

Ali's back stiffened. ''I don't know what you're talking about, but I don't appreciate being addressed in that fashion.''

What would Robert do if he were here? The answer made Matt slam his hand down on the table, his jaw tightening into a stubborn set. ''Well, I won't allow it.''

Matt realized too late that his voice was loud enough to make the other patrons in the café turn and stare at him. But that was the least of his worries; a pair of indignant gray eyes were about to bore a hole through him.

''I beg your pardon?'' she asked. Her tone was chilly enough to freeze lava.

''I said I won't let you do it,'' Matt said flatly. He leveled what was meant to be a cool gaze at her, but a slight twitch in his jaw gave away his effort to control his temper. "I was Robert's best friend, and there's no way I'm going to let his sister pull a damn fool stunt she'll regret for the rest of her life."

Ali eyed him icily. "I'm an adult, and I'll do as I darn well please. Who the heck do you think you are, telling me what I can and can't do?"

What a mule-headed female! Matt leaned across the table in what he hoped was an intimidating fashion. "I'll tell you who I am. I'm a person who owes it to Robert to keep his sister from marrying a con artist who's only interested in her inheritance," he said tersely.

There! He'd said it—although not as delicately as he'd originally intended. He watched her eyes widen, and decided to press on while he had her attention. "If I have to truss you up and take you across the state border on Saturday to prevent you from making the mistake of a lifetime, I'll damn wel' do it."

Ali stared at him for a moment, her eyes round and her mouth open in a perfect little "o." Then, to Matt's total discomfiture, she burst into laughter.

"I don't see what's so funny about this," he snapped. "If you don't think I'm serious, just try me."

Ali only laughed harder—so hard, in fact, that she clutched her stomach and doubled over, laughing until tears rolled down her cheeks.

Matt watched her in confusion. Of all the reactions he'd imagined she might have, he'd never thought of this one. He was vaguely aware that the entire café was regarding them with undisguised interest. Was she hysterical? Maybe she needed medical attention. Matt was wondering if he should call for help when she pulled herself together enough to speak.

"You think I'm going to marry Derrick Atchison," she finally gasped. The words sent her into another round of mirth.

Matt eyed her suspiciously. "What am I supposed to think?"

She gripped the edge of the table and succumbed to another fit of giggles.

Matt reached across and grabbed her hand. It felt warm and soft and surprisingly slight under his fingers. Touching her made him adopt a gentler tone. "Are you saying you're *not* marrying Derrick?"

Ali's eyes fell on her captured hand. The physical contact seemed to have a sobering effect on her. "Of course not. Susan Connors is marrying Hank. I'm going to be the maid of honor, and Derrick is the best man."

Matt knit his brows together. "But I distinctly heard Hank say you and Derrick are walking down the aisle together."

"We are—after the ceremony, behind Susan and Hank." Ali's voice once again had that be-patient-with-the-idiot quality to it. She withdrew her hand, picked up her napkin and dabbed at her cheeks. "The maid of honor and the best man always follow the bridal couple out of the church. We practiced it at the rehearsal last night."

Matt wished he could slither under the table. He squirmed on the vinyl booth and clenched his knuckles on the tabletop. "I see. I thought—well, it's pretty obvious what I thought."

Ali reached over and patted his arm. "Actually, it's very sweet of you to be so concerned," she said softly, "even if you were awfully high-handed. But you and I need to get two things straight if we're going to work together. One—I happen to have a pretty good head on my shoulders, regardless of what you may have heard. And two—I don't need another big brother."

Matt's head jerked to attention. "Whoa. Back up a moment. Did you say work together?"

Ali nodded. "I intended to come talk to you next week, but since the subject has come up, we might as well discuss it now."

"Discuss what now?" Matt's orderly life suddenly seemed to be careening out of control.

Ali took a sip of her ice tea, then reached for the sugar. "Well, Robert left me his half of your company. My attorney tells me that most of the assets are tied up in the Victorian Village housing development that's now under construction."

"Right," Matt said cautiously. "So?"

"So it doesn't strike me as fair that I'll receive half the profits without doing any of the work." Ali calmly opened a packet of sugar and poured it into her glass. "I've got some great ideas for the project and I've moved back to Hillsboro to help you with it."

She couldn't have shocked him more if she'd dropped a bomb in his lap. In fact, Matt felt like she'd done just that. "Now wait just a cotton-picking minute," he began. *Easy, Jordan—proceed with caution*, a little voice inside him warned. *Strong-arm tactics will just get her back up again.*

Matt drew a deep breath and deliberately lowered his voice. "That really isn't necessary," he said with feigned nonchalance. "Robert completed his portion of the work when he designed the homes."

"But I *want* to help," Ali said. "I'm an interior designer, Matt, and I've always wanted to work on one of Robert's projects. He told me that we would someday. This was his last project, so it's the only 'someday' I've got."

"But...but..." Matt sputtered. Her words were striking pure terror in his heart. He searched for another way to dissuade her. "What about your job in Dallas?"

"I quit," Ali told him.

Matt barely stifled a groan. Great. Just great. She was really serious about this.

"I'd gotten tired of the pace of the city and I missed my old friends, anyway," she continued, "so I decided to move back to Hillsboro. Since Robert left his house to me, it seemed like a logical decision."

Logical? By whose definition?

Ali glanced at her watch. "Oh, dear—I'm nearly late for the bridesmaid's luncheon. Look, I'll be home later today and most of tomorrow if you want to discuss this some more. Feel free to drop by. Otherwise, I'll see you at the office on Monday." She flashed him a smile, then she was gone.

Matt stared after her, feeling like he'd been hit by a cyclone. He watched her sweep out of the café in a whirl of black and red, thinking that a cyclone was an all too accurate analogy. After all, what she proposed would cut a swath of chaos through his well-ordered life.

There was a phrase to describe his situation, he thought glumly—a phrase weathermen used to describe the part of the country most frequently hit by destructive twisters.

Tornado Alley.

Better make that Tornado Ali. Matt heaved a sigh and raked a hand through his hair. Whichever way he spelled it, he was definitely in for a rough time.

Chapter Two

"Okay, Flipper—ready? Go get it, boy!"

Ali flung the miniature Frisbee disc. The small black and white dog scampered through the dry leaves, leapt high in the air and caught the toy in his teeth.

Ali grinned and clapped her hands, her thick wool mittens muffling the sound. The little dog darted back to her and plopped the toy at her feet, barking sharply and wagging his tail. Ali bent and petted the animal as she picked up the disc.

"Good catch! You really love this game, don't you, fella? Okay, here we go again. Ready...set...go!" Ali drew back her arm and again hurled the disc. To her dismay, this time it landed on the slope of the roof.

"Drats!" she exclaimed. Flipper stood on his hind legs and whined.

"Don't worry, boy," she crooned to her pet. "We'll get it down. I think there's a ladder in the garage." Ali headed back to the house, the frozen grass crunching under her feet as the little dog followed at her heels.

She found the ladder resting against the wall where she remembered it. As she bent to lift it, she noticed a box beside it on the concrete floor. She pulled up the flap and peered inside.

Drafting tools. The sight made Ali's eyes mist over and a lump formed in her throat.

She picked up a slide rule and reverently ran her mittened hand along the length of it, her heart aching to see the instruments her brother had loved so much and used so well boxed and forgotten in the garage.

This wasn't the first time she'd been hit by a sudden, overwhelming wave of grief. She'd felt the same thing when she walked into the house—a house Robert had designed, a home filled with his furniture, a place that so strongly reminded her of her brother that she could almost hear him laugh in the other room.

Why hadn't she come to visit him here when he was alive? He'd begged her to come last summer.

Ali gently placed the slide rule back in the box. She knew exactly why she hadn't come, and she might as well admit it: she'd wanted to avoid Robert's well-intentioned advice on how to live her life.

Ali sighed and sat back on her heels. She'd adored her big brother, but he'd been her exact opposite. Practical to a fault, he never made a move without carefully weighing every conceivable consequence. Ali, on the other hand, preferred to tackle life head-on, attracting mishaps like a magnet.

Ali sighed again. It was true that everything she touched somehow took an unexpected turn, but that didn't mean she wasn't fully capable of managing her own life. Unfortunately, she'd never convinced her brother of that fact. He'd felt it was his duty to point out the error of her ways and he hadn't abandoned the task once she'd become an adult.

She wiped a tear from her cheek, the mitten rough against her skin. Robert had never known how badly his criticisms had hurt, how much she'd yearned for his acceptance and approval. In fact, the desire to earn his respect was part of the reason she'd moved to Dallas as soon as she'd earned a degree at the local college. She'd hoped to prove herself in the big city—and she'd done a pretty good job of it, too, she thought with a modest burst of pride. In the past five years as an interior designer with a major furniture store, she'd received three promotions.

But her secret plan had been shattered by her brother's death. She'd always harbored the dream that someday she'd work with Robert and show him that she was capable, competent and mature. If she could do that, maybe she could finally believe, deep down where it counted, that she wasn't an overgrown child like her mother—that she was strong and independent, that she could function on her own, that her ideas had weight and merit.

Now her only chance to work on one of Robert's projects was the housing development Matt was building.

Ali chewed the inside of her lip worriedly at the thought of Matt. They hadn't gotten off to a very good start. He seemed to be laboring under the misguided notion that she needed a surrogate big brother. Judging from the way he'd acted and his remarks about her being unpredictable, her reputation had preceded her.

She blew a stray curl from her forehead in a sharp puff of air as frustration tightened her chest. She'd long ago accepted the fact that an extraordinary number of odd things seemed to happen around her, but other people sometimes had a hard time adjusting to it. Especially rigidly structured, plan-every-detail types like Matt Jordan.

Well, she'd just have to try extra hard to appear as normal as possible around him. She'd present her plan in a professional, businesslike manner on Monday, and hopefully he'd agree with her ideas.

Ali's mouth firmed into a determined line. He had to; this was her only opportunity to pay back the brother who'd stepped into a parental role when their father had died, who'd mowed the piano teacher's lawn in exchange for her lessons, who'd held a before-school paper route and an after-school restaurant job to pay for braces for her teeth.

Ali rose to her feet and dusted off her knees. Robert had viewed this project as the most important one of his career, and she was determined to help make it a reality.

A surge of energy flowed through her as she thought of her plans. "Come on, Flipper," she said to her pet, picking up the ladder and heading for the garage door. "Let's go get your toy."

The cold wind invigorated her face and lifted her spirits. With Flipper jumping excitedly at her heels, she dragged the ladder across the grass and leaned it against the house.

The moment it was set in place, the little dog dashed up the rungs.

"Flipper! Oh, my gosh—what are you doing?"

Ali watched helplessly as her pet scampered up the ladder. "Come back down here right now," she ordered. *"Flipper!"*

But it was too late. Flipper was already on the roof, picking his way across the thick wood shingles toward the disc. Ali gazed in horror as he clamped his teeth around the toy and stretched his head over the edge to look down at her, wagging his stumpy tail. Do dogs get dizzy? she wondered wildly.

"Don't move! *Stay!*" she shouted.

"Why? What's the matter?" an alarmed masculine voice responded.

Ali jerked her head in the direction of the voice and saw Matt entering the backyard, his hand frozen on the gate latch. "Not you—my dog. He's on the roof!" She pointed up at Flipper.

Matt craned his neck and stared up. Sure enough, a tiny black and white dog trotted along the edge of the overhang, a red disc grasped in its jaws. Matt blinked in disbelief. The mutt sat in the rain gutter, looked straight at him and growled.

Matt groaned. He'd come over here to straighten things out, figuring he and Ali could have a quiet, rational conversation. He should have known better. With all the normal, sane people in the world, why did his partner have to be related to a complete lunatic?

From the corner of his eye, Matt saw Ali head toward the ladder. Alarm raced through him and he quickly stepped in front of her, blocking her path. "What the hell are you doing?" he demanded.

"Going up after him."

"No." Matt's tone brooked no room for argument. He'd heard enough about Ali's mishaps to shudder at the thought of her climbing a ladder. "I'll go up. Better yet, why don't you just call him?"

"I'm afraid he'll jump."

The thought struck Matt as ludicrous, but the worried furrow between her brows made him repress his urge to smile. "Unless he's some sort of rare kamikaze breed, Ali, there's no way that dog is going to hurl himself off the roof."

"You don't know Flipper like I do!"

She's even nuttier than I imagined, Matt thought as he peered up at the mongrel. The little beast was sitting on the eave directly above them, thumping its sorry excuse of a tail. Matt reached up his arm and gestured toward the ladder. "Come on, fella. Here's the ladder—come on down. Here, boy," Matt coaxed.

"Don't encourage him!" Ali snapped.

"I'm telling you, there's no way that dog is going to jump." Matt turned his attention back to Flipper and gave an encouraging whistle.

Flipper immediately dropped the Frisbee disc, yapped twice and hurled himself off the roof, executing a neat flip in mid-air.

Matt reflexively dived for the dog, hitting the ground in a way that would have made his old college baseball coach proud. He cautiously opened one eye to find a warm, furry bundle squirming in his arms.

"Flipper! Oh, sweetie, I'm so glad you're okay!"

Matt opened his other eye to see Ali kneeling beside him. He caught a whiff of her perfume, something enticingly faint and soft and warm. The scent added to his overall confusion. She took the wriggling dog from his arms and cradled the creature to her chest.

"H-he jumped," Matt mumbled, raising himself cautiously on one elbow and inventorying his body parts. His backside hurt like the dickens, but otherwise he seemed okay. He slowly hauled himself to his feet.

"I warned you he might. Are you all right?" Still clutching the dog in one arm, Ali turned to Matt and began dusting him off.

Matt again inhaled her intriguing scent as she brushed the back of his jacket. He felt a sudden, irrational compulsion to get closer to her just to smell her better. Realizing he was on dangerous ground, Matt warily backed away. "I'm sure I will be once you tell me what just happened here."

"I was trying to get the toy off the roof and Flipper went up the ladder." Ali nuzzled the animal under her chin and Flipper responded by licking her cheek.

Matt eyed the dog suspiciously. As far as he could tell, it looked like an everyday, run-of-the-mill mutt. "So what's the explanation for the flying back flip action?"

"Flipper used to be a circus performer." Ali stroked the dog's head. "He knows lots of tricks. The problem is, I don't know what all of them are."

"Uh-huh. I see," said Matt. His tone implied he didn't see at all. "And just how did you happen to end up with a circus dog as a house pet?"

"His trainer took him to the SPCA. He said he was too much trouble." Ali shook her head. "Can you believe a person would give away a sweet little dog like this for a silly reason like that?"

Was she for real? Matt shook his head at her. "It defies the imagination," he said dryly.

"Well, thanks for catching him," Ali said. "You probably saved Flipper's life."

Matt was about to make a sarcastic reply, but her smile was so warm that the words stuck in his throat. He found himself staring at her, taking in her wind-chapped cheeks, her tousled hair and the expression of unabashed affection lighting her eyes as she cuddled her dog. It was enough to make him envy the mutt.

"You had a new trick to show me, hmm?" Ali cooed to the animal. "You're just full of surprises, aren't you?"

"You can say that again," Matt muttered, but he wasn't thinking of the dog. His eyes were riveted on her lips as she

ROBIN WELLS 27

kissed the top of Flipper's head. He swallowed hard and found himself responsively running his tongue over his own mouth. "I'd better put the ladder in the garage before Flipper decides to give a repeat performance," he said abruptly.

"Good idea. Thanks."

But Matt didn't immediately move. He was oddly mesmerized by the motion of her fingers stroking Flipper's fur.

"I'll go make us some hot tea. Just come on in when you're done." She looked up and smiled at him, and Matt felt his mouth go dry. Her smile was like a burst of midsummer sunshine, and Matt found himself wanting to bask in it.

With an effort, he pulled his eyes away. "Okay." He headed for the ladder, pausing to pick up the miniature disc from the lawn.

Watch out, Jordan, he warned himself caustically. She's already got one male doing back flips for her. She doesn't need another.

Chapter Three

Ali closed the kitchen door and set Flipper on the Mexican tile floor. "Well, boy, we certainly made quite an impression," she told her pet as she peeled off her mittens. She stuffed them in her coat pocket, then pulled off her parka and hung it on the coatrack in the corner. "Not exactly the calm, normal image I hoped to project, but an impression nonetheless."

Lifting the teakettle from the stove, Ali turned to the sink and gazed out the window.

Matt was walking toward the garage with the ladder slung under his arm as though it were weightless. Ali stared, engrossed by his easy, masculine grace. Robert had told her Matt often worked side-by-side with his work crew, and his physique certainly testified to the fact. He had the build of a man accustomed to using his muscles. His shoulders were broad and straight, and his thighs were so muscular that they strained against the denim fabric of his jeans with every step.

Whatever else he might be, there was no denying that Matt Jordan was one fine figure of a man. Ali watched his breath cloud the cold air and found the sight somehow sensual. He looked warm and male and . . . hot-blooded.

Ali realized the kettle was overflowing. "Keep your mind on business," she scolded herself, turning off the faucet and pouring out some of the water before she placed the kettle on the burner.

After all, business was undoubtedly the reason for Matt's unexpected appearance. She needed to be focusing her energies on how to best convince him to let her play an active role in his company instead of admiring his biceps.

The thought made Ali frown as she turned and drew two mugs from the cabinet. Matt was evidently impatient to finish their discussion. It had been a mistake to mention her plans to him in the café, she thought ruefully. Now she wasn't going to have the opportunity to present her ideas in a professional setting. Not to mention the fact that the incident outdoors had done nothing to foster the image of a competent, collected businesswoman she'd so hoped to project the next time she saw him.

Well, she could correct some of the damage by showing him documents to support her ideas. Surely facts and figures would convince Matt that she could make a positive contribution to the project.

Ali hurried into the living room, pulled a file out of a leather folder and strategically placed it on the living room coffee table. "There," she murmured.

By the time she heard Matt open the door a few minutes later, she felt more than ready to present her case.

But then he stepped into the kitchen, filling the room, making it suddenly seem both smaller and warmer. A primal awareness of Matt as a man skittered through her, making her pulse lurch erratically.

Annoyed at herself, she stepped toward him. "Let me take your coat."

Matt shrugged off his jacket and handed it to her. She carried it across the room to the coatrack, inhaling the scent of leather and shaving cream.

A fleeting fantasy raced through her mind—the image of Matt stripped to the waist, his face lathered, his biceps bulging as he wielded a razor.

She turned back toward him and her gaze snagged on the dark hair peeking out of his unbuttoned shirt collar. Her cheeks burned and she averted her eyes. She couldn't afford to indulge in ridiculous daydreams—not when her whole future hung in the balance. Especially not when the daydreams left her feeling as rattled as a key chain.

She ran her hands along the sides of her slacks to dry her damp palms, determined to get her thoughts back on track. "I've put some water on for tea," she said. "But if you like, I can make some coffee or get you a soft drink or make some hot chocolate..."

"Tea will be fine." Matt lounged against the counter and stretched out his legs. "Can I help with anything?"

The question took Ali by surprise. After his Neanderthal behavior at the restaurant, she hadn't figured him for the domestically helpful type. "I've almost gotten everything together," she said. "Why don't you go on into the living room?"

He pushed off the counter. "Want me to build a fire?"

"Sure. That would be nice." Ali drew a sigh of relief as he ambled through the doorway. Now that he was out of the kitchen, she could breathe again.

Ali pulled the sugar bowl from the cabinet and placed it on a wicker tray, then took a lemon from the refrigerator. Peering into the living room, she saw Matt kneeling in front of the fireplace, expertly arranging a stack of logs.

Where the heck were the knives? She rummaged through a drawer, then yanked open two more.

She hadn't unpacked her kitchen utensils yet and wasn't familiar with Robert's. For that matter, she wasn't familiar with anything in this house. It occurred to Ali that even though Robert's insurance had paid off the mortgage and she owned the home outright, she really didn't feel at home here.

Ali glanced back into the living room. Matt certainly didn't seem to have that problem. She watched him locate a box of matches in the bookcase with easy familiarity and expertly light the fire. If I were in charge of finding matches, we could have frozen to death, she thought wryly.

Ali finally found a knife and quickly sliced the lemon into wedges. She peeked back in the living room as she arranged them on a small plate. Matt was settled into a wing-backed chair, his leather cowboy boots propped on the coffee table. He looked right at home.

Matt must have visited Robert here often, she thought. A twinge of regret again coursed through her that she hadn't seen her brother at home in his dream house.

A home that Matt built. The thought startled her. Of course—why hadn't she realized that before? Robert had designed it, but Matt would have been the one to actually oversee its construction. It was the way their partnership had operated.

Ali grabbed a bag of cookies and threw a few on a plate. It was somehow disconcerting to realize that Matt knew intimate details about the place where she lived—the depth of the bathtub, how long she could stay in the shower before she ran out of hot water, the view from the bedroom....

Why am I thinking about Matt and the bedroom?

Ali gave herself a mental shake. This behavior was totally unlike her. If she was going to be the epitome of poise and professionalism as she intended, she couldn't afford to have her thoughts traveling down such dangerously distracting paths.

She picked up the tray, fixed a bright smile on her face and headed for the living room. "The tea will be ready in a moment. Would you care for a cookie?"

"No, thanks." Matt's eyes followed her as she set the tray on the coffee table and seated herself on the camelback sofa across from him. The knowledge that he was watching her made her uncharacteristically edgy. She was relieved when Flipper jumped in her lap, and she scratched the little dog's head, glad to have something to do with her hands.

Matt pulled his feet from the table and sat up straight in the chair. "Ali, I came by to continue our discussion. We need to get this thing settled." He leaned forward and cleared his throat. "Look, I'm sorry if I came on a little strong earlier."

That was an understatement. Ali generously decided to let it slide.

"I've been giving this situation some thought, and it dawned on me what you're after."

"What I'm after?" she echoed, furrowing her brow. She had no idea what he was talking about, but she didn't like the sound of it.

Matt nodded. His eyes bore a knowing gleam. "I don't blame you a bit. In your shoes, I'd be exactly the same way."

Ali regarded him quizzically. "What way is that? I'm afraid I'm not following you."

Matt's lips curled into a tight smile that didn't reach his eyes. "There's no need to play coy. I understand your concerns, and I'm willing to do whatever it takes to reassure you that the company is being properly managed. If you like, I can let your attorney look at the books to set your mind at ease."

What on earth was he talking about? The fire crackled and hissed, and Ali bristled. She didn't like the inference that she was somehow being underhanded. "I've never played coy in my life," she informed him, "and I don't have any concerns about your management abilities."

Matt shook his head, dismissing her comment with a wave of his hand. "If the situation were reversed, I'd be looking for a reason to keep an eye on things, too. After all, we don't know each other very well, and it's only natural that you'd want to look out for your own interests. But you really don't have to go to such lengths to keep me honest." Another taut smile tugged at the corners of his mouth. "Robert was my best friend, and I'm not going to cheat his little sister. I'll be happy to do whatever I can to reassure you of that fact. If you like, I can submit copies of all checks issued on the company account to your attorney or to any accountant you care to designate."

"You don't need to do that," Ali repeated. "Robert trusted you, so why shouldn't I? That isn't why I want to be involved in the company."

Matt eyed her skeptically. "Then why the heck do you?"

He thinks I'm only interested in keeping an eye on my inheritance. The realization rankled; how unfair of him to assume her motives were mercenary! She'd known he was the practical sort, but was he so unfeeling, so motivated purely by facts and figures and tangible things that he thought everyone else was, too? Ali opened her mouth to protest, then abruptly shut it again.

Getting on the defensive won't advance your cause. She silently warned herself. Besides, what did she expect him to think? He didn't know her from Adam. She needed to explain her motives to get him to listen to her ideas. He might think she was foolish, but it was a risk she had to take.

Ali put the dog on the floor and clasped her fingers tightly in her lap. "I'll tell you why. This project was Robert's dream, and I want to play a part in making it come true."

Matt's tawny eyes took her measure. "What do you even know about this project?"

"I was with him when he hit on the idea. He was visiting me in Dallas and we were browsing through an antique store. All of a sudden his face lit up and he asked me what I thought of the idea of building an entire community of Victorian-style homes."

Matt nodded, his face impassive. At least he appeared to be paying attention.

"I told him I thought it sounded terrific." She scooted forward on the sofa, eager to convince him. "Since I was there at the conception of this development, Matt, I feel like I have a stake in how it turns out. Besides, I've always wanted to work on a project with Robert, and this is my only chance." To her embarrassment, her eyes filled with tears, and she furiously tried to blink them back. Talking about her brother still made her emotional, but the last thing she wanted to do was stage a messy scene in front of Matt. He'd never take her seriously if he thought she was an emotional wreck.

Through her tear-muddled eyes, she watched him stand. For one terrible moment, she thought he was going to walk out on her. Instead, he crossed the room and sat beside her, lifting both of her hands in his. The tender, sympathetic gesture caught her by surprise, and she stared down at their entwined hands as if they were alien objects. His palms were warm and slightly callused, his fingers strong and brown, his nails short and clean. She was suddenly aware that dusk had fallen and the room was nearly dark except for the light from the fire.

"Look, Ali, I know how important this project was to Robert—and I can see that it's important to you. It's important to me, too, and not just for business reasons." Matt paused and Ali ventured a glance up at his face. In the soft light, his eyes were the color of hot cocoa, and just as warm and soothing. Her heart thudded in her chest and she wondered how a man could be so comforting and so unnerving at the same time.

Matt's thumbs moved across her palms. "Robert was my best friend. It may sound corny, but I see this development as a way of keeping a part of Robert alive. I guess I view it as a memorial to his talent."

There was more to Matt than she'd realized—a lot more. She gazed down at their fingers, still threaded together, and felt a sense of connectedness weave its way between them. The tightness in her chest that always gripped her when she thought of Robert eased a bit.

Matt had genuinely cared for her brother, she realized. He not only understood how she felt, he felt the same way. He shared her loss, and he shared her goal. There was a bond between them, a bond stronger than their differences.

The thought startled her, and she jumped as a log shifted on the fire. She looked up at Matt's face and in the warm depths of his eyes, she saw that he, too, felt the emotional connection. He squeezed her fingers and an undeniable tug of attraction coursed through her. She leaned toward him, drawn by some invisible, magnetic force. The firelight, the faint scent of smoke and Matt's warm hands wrapped around hers somehow smudged the edges of reality. Her gaze took in the fine lines at the corners of his eyes, the faint shadow of his clean-shaven beard, the deep cleft in his chin. She was studying the sensuous curve of his lips, wondering how they would feel on hers, when she saw them move and realized he was talking.

"What you need to understand, is that I have a very well-organized, well-planned program already in place to make that happen." Matt's voice was low and gentle and so appealing that it took her a second to comprehend what he was saying. "I don't want to hurt your feelings, but I've got all the bases covered. There isn't a role for you in this. To be absolutely frank, you'd just be in the way."

The words struck Ali like a splash of cold water. She stiffened and pulled away, withdrawing her hands from his. "You're underestimating the contribution I can make."

Matt rose from the chair and strode to the fireplace. He braced his hands against the thick oak mantel for a moment, then turned toward her. "What do you know about home building, Ali? Would you know if the foundation was level, or if the lumber had too many knot holes?"

Ali smoothed her hair as she tried to smooth her raw, ruffled nerves. "Well, no."

Matt folded his arms across his chest. "Would you know if the proper type and amount of insulation had been installed?"

"That isn't my area of expertise."

"If the electrical contractor is taking shortcuts, would you be able to tell? If the plumber tries to use pipes of an inferior quality, would you know the difference?"

"Of course not," Ali said stiffly. "I'm an interior designer, not a general contractor."

"My point exactly." Matt sat back down in the chair with an air of finality, his expression clearly indicating he considered the issue settled.

Ali felt the blood rise in her face. It was her turn to stand and pace. "If you don't mind, I'd like to ask *you* a few questions," she said. "What color are you going to paint the rooms?"

From the startled look on his face, Ali guessed that he hadn't even given the issue a thought. "White, I guess," he said.

"Every room of every house?"

"Well, I suppose so." His voice had a slight defensive edge to it. "Not stark white—more of an off-white. Why not? It's a nice, neutral color. I've used it in lots of spec homes and people seem to like it just fine."

"These aren't your standard, modern spec homes," Ali informed him briskly. "And white walls throughout are totally inappropriate to Victorian-style architecture. What type of flooring are you planning to use?"

His eyes became guarded. "Carpeting. Linoleum in the kitchen and bathrooms."

"No hardwood floors? Not even in the foyers?"

Ali could tell the answer from his expression and didn't bother to wait for his reply. "What type of ceiling molding are you going to use?" she continued.

"I'm, uh, not planning to install any ceiling moldings."

A little thrill of righteous indignation ran through her. "Then I don't suppose you've thought about wainscoting, either."

Matt rose to his feet again and confronted her at the mantel. "Now, look, these things cost money," he protested. "You're talking about luxury items that can really add up."

"They're also the type of things that buyers are willing to spend more money to get." Ali picked up her folder from the coffee table and pulled out a trade magazine. She opened it to a marked page and handed the publication to him. "Here," she said, thrusting it at him. "Read this."

Matt scanned the article and handed it back to her. "Okay, so one study proved that home buyers in one part of the country like certain extras. Fine. That doesn't necessarily translate into what's going to work with home buyers in Hillsboro, Oklahoma."

Ali felt her temper rise. She waved the folder in front of him. "For your information, I've got several reports that all say the same thing."

Matt shrugged. "It still doesn't mean it would work here."

Ali glared at him, her hands on her hips. "Why on earth wouldn't it? And what about the fact that homes with these features sell forty percent faster?"

Matt waved a hand dismissively. "Look, I'm sure all these niceties would be ... nice, but it's out of the question. We're financed to the limit. It's going to take every cent of what we've already borrowed to build the homes the way they're planned."

He was completely close-minded, she thought hotly. He wasn't willing to even entertain the possibility that she was right. She must be out of her mind to think Matt was attractive. He was exactly the sort of man she'd always vowed to avoid: bossy, obstinate, rigid and stubborn.

She struggled to maintain her composure. "What if I come up with additional financing?"

Matt's arms were crossed and his lips were set in a firm line. Everything about his demeanor told Ali he considered the subject closed. "Even if you could talk the bank into increasing the loan, I'm not willing to incur any more indebtedness."

"Is money your only objection?"

The question seemed to stop Matt short. He raised a wary eyebrow, and Ali was sure he suspected a trick. "Yes," he said after a moment. "And it's the only one I need."

"All right." Ali nodded her head as if they'd struck a deal. A plan had formed in her mind, but she wasn't about to discuss it. It was always easier to apologize than to get permission.

Matt continued to eye her suspiciously. "All right what?"

"Just—all right."

The teapot whistled in the kitchen and Flipper gave two sharp barks. Ali suppressed a smile as she watched Matt closely. She couldn't wait to see his smug composure given another jolt.

Just as she knew he would, her little dog bolted into the air and threw himself into a perfect back flip. To her gratification, Matt's eyes grew wide with shock.

His jaw open, he turned to Ali. "What in blazes . . ."

Ali laughed. "Whenever he hears any type of bell or whistle, he flips. It's how he got his name."

Flipper wagged his tail proudly and Ali escaped to the kitchen to grab the kettle. She was glad of the distraction. The tension between them had grown thick enough to cut with a knife.

What an impossible man! He was a Class-A control freak and as stubborn as they came. She was going to have to tread carefully. She had a feeling that once Matt dug in his heels on an issue, it would take a bulldozer to make him budge.

Well, she knew a thing or two about bulldozing her way through an issue, too. Matt Jordan might not know it yet, but he had met his match.

Chapter Four

"Oh, Ali, it's gorgeous!" Susan Connors exclaimed. She lifted the lacy, blush-colored teddy from its nest of tissue paper and held it up in front of her. "I love it—and so will Hank." She wriggled her eyebrows suggestively.

Ali glanced at her wristwatch and grinned at her friend. "Well, in just nine hours, it'll be legal to find out."

Susan smiled back. "I swear, Ali, this is the longest day of my life. Everything's all done and there's nothing to do but wait for seven o'clock to arrive. Whatever made me decide to have an evening wedding?"

"Your streak of romanticism. You wanted moonbeams and candlelight, remember?" Ali reminded her. She picked up the coffeepot and carefully filled two mugs with the steaming brew. "Besides, the afternoon will fly by. You'll be busy at the hairdresser's, then you'll take a long, luxurious bath and get dressed—and before you know it, you'll be Mrs. Hank Townsend."

"You always manage to make me feel better," Susan said fondly. "I'm so glad you moved back to Hillsboro, Ali. I've really missed having you around."

"I've missed you, too," Ali replied. She crossed the kitchen and handed her friend a cup of coffee, then sank into a chair across from her in the breakfast nook. "It feels good to be back. Besides, you couldn't get married without me. Remember how we vowed when we were little girls that we'd always do everything together?"

Susan nodded, her short auburn curls bouncing up and down. "That's right. We'd better get to work and get you married soon or we'll fall out of sync."

Ali grimaced. "I'm afraid I don't have very good luck with men."

"That's because you haven't gotten involved with the right one yet," Susan reassured her.

"I think it's more than that. I've done a lot of thinking lately, and I've come to the conclusion that men think I'm a pushover."

Susan's eyebrows shot up and she leaned forward with avid interest. "Oh, really? When did this happen?"

Trust Susan to put a sexual twist on her statement—especially since she knew Ali had limited experience in that department. Ali shot her friend a censoring look. "I simply meant it seems like every man I encounter wants to run my life."

Susan smiled at Ali fondly. "They probably view your life as a challenge. You have to admit that an incredible number of odd things happen around you."

"I know," Ali sighed, fingering the handle of her coffee mug. "My life is like a continual episode of 'I Love Lucy.'"

Susan laughed. "But there's one major difference. Most of the situations aren't your fault. You're not careless or reckless or crazy. You're just . . . destined for excitement."

Ali smiled. "With tact like that, you belong in the diplomatic corps. But I might as well face it, Suze . . . my aura of excitement isn't exactly conducive to romance. Men either immediately run the other direction or try to take me firmly in hand."

Susan's eyebrows roguishly rose.

Ali rolled her eyes. "I should know better than to discuss this with a woman about to go on a honeymoon."

Laughing, Susan reached across the table to pat her hand. "Seriously, Ali, I think you're a little paranoid."

Ali gazed down at her coffee mug. "Maybe so. I guess I'm afraid I'll end up like my mother." She looked up at Susan earnestly. "After all, Robert ended up just as domineering as my father—you know how he took over trying to run my life right after Dad died. So if he's a chip off the old block, maybe I'm a chip off the old doormat." Ali shook her head. "I loved my parents, but I don't want a marriage like theirs, Susan. I'd rather be on my own."

"You're not at all like your mother that way," Susan said gently. "She *wanted* your dad to call the shots. He was a lot older than she was, and I think she saw him as a father figure instead of an equal." Susan leaned forward. "You're completely different. You've been living on your own in the city ever since you got out of college. You've got a career and you're self-supporting. Why, I don't think I know a more independent woman than you." Susan gave Ali's hand another pat. "The right man is out there. In fact, he might be right under your nose. What about Matt?"

Ali stared at her friend. "Matt? You've got to be kidding. If you looked up the word bossy in the dictionary, you'd probably see his picture. First he behaves like an overprotective big brother—"

"Actually, I thought it was sweet of Matt to try to warn you about Derrick," Susan interjected. "And he's right. Derrick might be Hank's closest living relative, but he's pure trouble and everyone in town knows it."

"Well, there's nothing sweet about the way Matt refuses to consider my ideas for the development," Ali grumbled.

"I'm sure you'll bring him around," Susan reassured her. "You may think you don't want a strong-minded man, Ali, but my guess is you'd be bored by anything less." Susan gave her a sly grin. "Robert thought you and Matt would be perfect for each other."

Ali stared at her friend. Her stomach gave a sudden lurch, as if she'd just gone over a hill at a high speed. "Robert *what?*"

"He thought you two might hit it off. That's why he was trying to get you to come back to Hillsboro last summer. He even enlisted my help to try to get you here."

Ali's head swam as she recalled the insistent phone calls she'd received from Robert and Susan. "Was Matt aware of this scheme?"

Susan shook her head. "No. He was as much in the dark as you. Robert knew you were both too stubborn to go along with any type of matchmaking plan."

"See what I mean about Robert trying to run my life?" Ali eyed her friend with mock indignation. "And you were going to help him!"

Susan shrugged. "Hank and Matt are friends, and I think he's really nice. Besides, you have to admit he's quite a hunk."

The fantasy of a shirtless Matt again filled Ali's mind. She certainly couldn't argue the point. "Well, I have no interest in getting involved with anyone anytime soon." Especially not the man who was Robert's selection. She'd loved her big brother, but she'd spent the last three years trying to establish her independence. It was high time she made her own decisions.

Susan picked up the teddy by its tiny spaghetti straps. The sunlight streamed through the transparent fabric. "Ali, any woman who would pick out lingerie like this is not totally disinterested in men." She raised an eyebrow. "And if I'm any judge of men, Matt Jordan is the kind who could properly appreciate an outfit like this."

"Susan—honestly!"

"And speak of the devil," Susan murmured as she gazed out the window. A mischievous grin lit her face. "Don't look now, but you've got company."

Ali followed her friend's gaze out to the patio. Matt was coming through the back gate, his arms laden with firewood. Ali's heart quickened at the sight of him, and she found herself annoyed at her physical response. It's nothing but a reaction to Susan's insinuations, she told herself. Even more likely, she was edgy because they hadn't resolved the partnership question. He'd left quickly after their discussion yesterday, evidently thinking the matter was settled. Ali knew it was anything but.

She watched him crouch and begin stacking logs on the meager remnants of her woodpile, irritated at the way her eyes were drawn to the snug fit of his faded jeans.

Determined not to sit and ogle the man, Ali rose and opened the back door. "Hi. The fire man cometh, I see."

Matt looked up and grinned, his even white teeth accentuating his tan. "Something like that. Robert and I used to take turns cutting firewood when we cleared our development sites and I noticed yesterday that you were running low."

It was a kind gesture, exactly the sort of thing Robert would have done for her if he'd been alive. And exactly the sort of thing she shouldn't allow Matt to do if she wanted him to think of her as an equal partner instead of a little sister in need of a guardian.

Ali folded her arms across her chest. "Thanks, but I'm afraid I can't accept it. I don't take charity, and since I'm not very handy with a chain saw, I won't be able to return the favor."

Matt gave an amused chuckle and straightened his back, shoving his hands into his fleece-lined denim jacket. "I didn't exactly expect that you would. But I cut too much wood—habit, I guess. I've got more than enough to see me through the next month, and it looks like you could use some."

Ali hesitated. There was no point in arguing over a gesture that was only meant to be neighborly. Maybe he was feeling apologetic about the way he'd so abruptly dismissed her suggestions yesterday. She shifted uneasily and gave a grudging nod, rubbing her hands along her arms. "Well, thanks. It was thoughtful of you."

Matt's grin crinkled the corners of his eyes in a way that made Ali's pulse race. "Don't mention it. I'll bring around a couple more loads from my truck."

"I'll help," Ali said suddenly. If she shared in the labor, she wouldn't feel so beholden to him.

"No need. It'll just take a few minutes. Besides, it looks like you've got company."

Ali followed his gaze over her shoulder and was startled to find Susan standing behind her in the doorway. She'd completely forgotten that her friend was there.

Susan's wide grin made Ali uneasy. She was afraid Matt would pick up on the fact they'd been talking about him from Susan's amused expression.

Ali surreptitiously elbowed her to knock it off. "Susan, I believe you know Matt Jordan?"

Ignoring Ali's warning glare, Susan stepped out of the doorway and continued to smile as she shook Matt's hand.

"Sure. Nice to see you, Matt."

"Good to see you, too," he replied. "Today's the big day, hmm?"

"Sure is." Susan beamed.

"Well, I'll see you and Hank this evening."

Ali looked at Susan in surprise. She hadn't mentioned that she'd invited Matt to the wedding. But then, she *had* said that Hank and he were friends, she reminded herself.

Matt was gazing intently at something inside the doorway and Ali turned to see what it was. She was mortified to see the teddy draped over the back of a chair.

Reflexively, she reached for it. Matt's gaze shifted from the silk in her hand up to her face. Their eyes locked for a second, then he looked away—but not before Ali caught a glimmer of speculation in his eyes.

He thought the skimpy undergarment was hers! Ali's face flamed with heat. It was ridiculous, but she somehow felt exposed—as though Matt had uncovered the fact that extravagant lingerie was her secret vice. What she wore under her clothes was nobody's business, least of all Matt Jordan's. And she certainly didn't want him thinking about it.

Matt cleared his throat. "If you ladies will excuse me, I'll go get another load of wood." He turned abruptly toward the gate with Flipper close behind.

Susan moved back inside and Ali closed the door behind her, brandishing the filmy garment. "Did you leave this in plain sight on purpose? He thinks it's mine!"

Susan gave an impish shrug. "I don't see what's so terrible. It'll just make him wonder what you look like in it."

"Just what I need," Ali moaned. "A business partner who won't take me seriously imagining me in racy lingerie."

Susan laughed, put the gift back in its box and pulled on her coat. "Thanks again for the present—and for offering a diversion from the prewedding jitters. I think I can make it until seven o'clock now."

Ali gave her friend a hug. In a few hours Susan would begin a new life—a life based on love and sharing and commitment. Ali's own life suddenly seemed sadly empty in comparison.

She couldn't help but feel a little wistful as she walked her friend to the door. "I'm glad you came by—even if you did see fit to make Matt think I look like Gypsy Rose Lee under my clothes," she teased softly.

"It never hurts to give a man a little something to think about," Susan blithely responded.

"I'd prefer to have Matt thinking about interior design."

Susan flashed a knowing smile as she breezed out the door. "Ulterior designs are much more interesting, Ali."

Matt rounded the corner with his third load of wood to find Ali walking toward him. Backlit by the sun, her hair gleamed around her face like a mahogany halo.

A ripple of attraction tightened his stomach and traveled lower. She had a fresh, unfussy, one-of-a-kind beauty that seemed to grow more pronounced each time he saw her. She also had a way of making ordinary, everyday clothing look extraordinarily seductive. Her jeans weren't tight, but they hugged her body in all the right places. Matt had a strong urge to do the same. His mind flickered to an image of her clad in that tidbit of an undergarment he'd glimpsed in the kitchen and his body gave a surge of response.

Easy, boy. She might look like an angel, but she'd give you pure hell. Hadn't she already managed to throw him for a loop every time he'd seen her? The last thing he needed was to get involved with a woman who attracted trouble like Pigpen collected dirt.

Matt dropped the wood on the ground beside her and shoved his hands into his pockets. "Did Susan leave?" he asked.

Ali nodded. "She's off to the beauty salon to begin her transformation into a bride." She studied the growing jumble of logs on the ground. "I really appreciate the wood, Matt."

"No problem. I'll bring around another couple of loads, then I'll stack it."

"I can handle the stacking."

"No need. Why don't you stay inside where it's warm and let me take care of it?"

"Because I'd rather stack wood." Her tone was insistent, almost combative. She knelt and began arranging logs on the woodpile.

Matt shrugged. If she really wanted to work out here in the freezing cold, he wouldn't try to stop her. "Suit yourself. I'll go get another load."

Matt puzzled over Ali's attitude as he headed for his pickup truck. He had the distinct impression he'd somehow offended her. Funny—she didn't seem like the militant women's lib type. He couldn't imagine why she'd be mad about a delivery of firewood. She must still be upset over the way he'd told her there was no place for her at the construction company.

Well, he could hardly blame her; he had to admit he hadn't been exactly tactful, Matt thought, rubbing his jaw ruefully. The truth was, he'd felt darn guilty over how he'd handled it; after all, she was Robert's sister, and he should have let her down a little easier. He'd dropped by with the wood this morning as a peace offering.

"Women!" Matt muttered, climbing into the bed of his truck and pushing some logs toward the tailgate. He'd never been very good at figuring them out. His ex-wife was proof enough of that. It had taken nearly a year of marriage before he'd realized her love of money far exceeded any love she claimed to have for him—and he'd only figured that out when she left him for a wealthy oilman forty years his senior.

The entire marriage had been a disaster from the word go, and he had no intention of making a mistake like that again. No, sirree; matrimony might be fine for some men—Hank, for example—but it wasn't for him. He loved women, but he had no intention of ever being in love with one again.

Women tended to complicate life too much, anyway. He liked to be able to plan things out and have things go according to plan, and he'd never met a woman yet who couldn't throw a kink into even the most thoroughly thought-out project.

He swung down from the truck and began loading his arms with logs. Ali was a prime example, he thought with a shake of his head. Every time he'd seen her, something bizarre had happened. Just thinking about her had a way of confusing him—and he'd found himself thinking about her far too often.

Well, he probably wouldn't have to deal with her much longer, he reasoned. Most likely she'd get bored with small town life in a few weeks and move back to Dallas. In the meantime, he'd do what he could to keep an eye on her and to reassure her the company was running smoothly.

Balancing a stack of logs so tall he had to crane his neck to see around it, Matt headed for the woodpile. The sight that greeted him as he rounded the corner stopped him dead in his tracks, causing him to nearly drop his load. Holy pajamas! Ali was leaning forward, her trim, shapely backside pointed pertly in the air, her jeans hugging every luscious curve. Matt swallowed hard. She was enough to make a bulldog pop his chain.

Oblivious of the heavy load in his arms, Matt stood stock-still and watched her place another log on the pile, all of his earlier resolve concerning her forgotten. Her short jacket rode up to reveal a waist that looked small enough to span with his hands. Matt's fingers itched to try it.

Thinking about it made his mouth run dry. He was so engrossed by the sight of her that when she suddenly stood up and stepped back, it took him by surprise. She bumped into him, knocking him off balance.

"Oh, I didn't know you were there!" she cried.

Matt struggled to retain his footing, but with the load of wood weighing down his arms, he couldn't regain his equilibrium. He tottered for an instant. Ali grabbed his arm, which threw him further off balance, and Matt tumbled to the ground in a jumble of logs.

"Matt! Are you all right?" He opened his eyes to find Ali leaning over him, her hair brushing his face. This was getting to be a habit.

"Owww," he responded. He reached a tentative hand for his head. When he withdrew it, his fingers were warm and sticky.

Ali hovered over him, her gray eyes wide and worried. "You're bleeding." She reached out and gently touched his hair. "Come inside and let me look at your head. We might need to get you to a doctor."

She helped him to his feet, then wrapped her slender arm around his waist. Matt reflexively draped an arm around her shoulder.

He felt light-headed all right, but he was pretty sure it wasn't due to the spill. Ali smelled delicious—like fresh flowers and herbal shampoo. Just for the moment, he decided not to fight the surge of pleasure coursing through him. He tilted his face slightly toward her neck to get a better whiff of her scent as he let her lead him into the house and down the hall to the bathroom.

"Sit down," she instructed, motioning to the side of the tub. He complied, noting it was the oversize Jacuzzi whirlpool tub. Robert had insisted that the spa bath would add to the house's resale value if he ever decided to sell. Sitting here watching Ali rummage through a drawer, Matt could think of an immensely more pleasurable and less practical use for the black marble beast.

"Here it is," she said, bending forward and reminding him of precisely what had caused the accident in the first place. She pulled out a bag of cotton balls and a bottle of antiseptic, then stepped close beside him. "Now, let me take a look at that cut."

Her breasts were at eye level, and the temperature in the room suddenly seemed to soar. Not knowing where to look, he closed his eyes as she touched his hair.

"Ouch!" he winced.

"Sorry." Her voice was soft, and she stroked his head apologetically, sending a tingle down his spine. "It doesn't look too bad—it's just a little cut. I think it's already stopped bleeding. Let me clean it up a bit."

Matt watched her pour something onto a cottonball and turn back toward him. "This will probably hurt a little," she warned.

She pulled his head against her breast, holding his face with one hand while she dabbed at the cut with the other. The pleasure of it far outweighed the slight discomfort. He sat perfectly still, barely daring to breathe, reveling in the feel of her cool palm on one cheek and her warm, firm breast on the other. He could hear her heart beat through the soft fabric of her sweater. He was fighting a powerful urge to reach out and pull her onto his lap, where a much stronger pain was developing.

Ali released his head and stepped back. "There. How does that feel?"

Terrible. We should go lie down until it goes away, he thought wildly.

"Fine," he said. Even to his ears, his voice sounded unusually husky. He made an effort to clear his throat and ended up coughing.

Ali eyed him with concern. "Are you sure you're okay? Maybe we should get your head X-rayed."

We should definitely get it examined, Matt told himself. What was he doing, thinking things like this about Robert's little sister? He must have knocked all the sense out his head with that fall.

Matt hauled himself to his feet. He needed to get out of here. Fast.

"I'm fine," he repeated. "Thanks for the first aid. Now, if you'll excuse me, I'd better be going."

Ali watched him stride from the bathroom. Only when she heard the back door close did she draw a deep breath.

Merciful heavens! She placed a hand protectively on her chest, precisely at the spot where his head had nestled against her. She could still feel the warmth of it imprinted on her breast, still feel the texture of his hair, still feel his eyes watching her every move. Something about touching him had rattled her down to her toenails. Her heart was pounding so loudly she was sure Matt must have heard it. At the same time, she was filled with an unaccustomed languor that made her feel like she was moving in slow motion.

What on earth was the matter with her?

Ali opened the drawer and began putting away the medical supplies. Susan's none-too-subtle suggestions about Matt had made her jumpy around him, that was all, she decided. It hadn't helped that the bathroom was unabashedly sensuous.

Well, she was going to have to get a grip on her emotions if she were going to work around Matt, she told herself sternly. Maybe increased exposure to him would make her immune to him. After all, what was that old saying? *Familiarity breeds contempt.*

So far, all familiarity seemed to be breeding was spontaneous combustion.

Ali gave herself a mental shake and left the room, firmly closing the door behind her. If only she could close the door on her thoughts about Matt as easily!

Chapter Five

If the parking lot was any indication, the wedding reception was already in full swing by the time Matt arrived at the Hillsboro Country Club. *Good,* he thought. He'd deliberately dawdled after the ceremony, not wanting to be among the first to arrive. He hated making small talk; by arriving late, maybe he could put in an appearance, congratulate Hank, and leave with a minimum amount of schmoozing. He was surprised to find a parking space right by the front door and maneuvered his Ford Taurus into it, hoping it was an omen that he could get in and out of the reception quickly.

Walking into the ballroom, Matt accepted a glass of champagne from a passing waiter and leaned against the wall. He watched the dancers glide around the floor to a Harry Connick, Jr. ballad and looked around for the bride and groom. Hank and Susan were swaying together in the corner. They appeared too wrapped up in each other to know who was or wasn't there. He might get out of here even sooner than he'd thought.

Which would definitely be a relief, Matt thought, running a finger under his collar and swallowing some champagne.

This whole setup made him uneasy. It reminded him too much of his own wedding ten years ago.

Just thinking about it made him scowl. He'd been fresh out of college, too young to know the difference between lust and love, and smitten with Elise's cool, polished exterior. He hadn't known it covered an equally cold heart. At the time, he'd mistaken her detached demeanor for serenity, her aloofness for poise. He'd thought she was the calm, collected type who shared his desire for a well-ordered life. Had he ever been wrong! All she desired was money—and when he didn't earn it fast enough to suit her, she was gone.

Well, she'd done him the biggest favor of his life by leaving, he thought. He only wished he'd had sense enough not to get involved with her in the first place. But he'd learned his lesson, and it was a mistake he intended not to repeat. No, indeed; never again would he get involved with an inappropriate woman.

Especially someone as completely inappropriate as Ali.

Matt took another sip of champagne and realized he'd unconsciously been scanning the room for her ever since he'd entered it. Regardless of what he might think of her, he had to admit that she'd looked ravishing at the wedding. He hadn't been able to keep his eyes off her during the ceremony—and who could blame him? That dress accented all the right spots, and her spots were definitely all right. Probably every man in the place had made the same observation.

The thought made him clench his jaw. Where the heck *was* she? Matt set his half-full glass of champagne on a table and headed to the far side of the ballroom.

He was only halfway across the room when he spotted her in the foyer, flanked by her fellow bridesmaids. All three girls were wearing identical dresses, but only Ali managed to make it look provocative.

As he'd figured, he hadn't been the only man to notice. Derrick Atchison and the other two male attendants were hovering over her as if she were a queen bee and they were her drones.

Matt tightened his jaw and began working his way through the crowd toward her. He lost sight of her for a moment, and when he spotted her again, he stopped dead in his tracks.

"Damn," he muttered, watching Derrick lead her by the hand to the dance floor. Matt was suddenly aware that the music had shifted to a sultry love song. He felt his chest constrict as Derrick placed his hand on her waist and pulled her close—far closer, Matt was certain, than was necessary.

Matt did a slow burn, his body tensing all over. Why was she even bothering to give the jerk the time of day? From their conversation earlier in the week, he knew she was aware of the creep's reputation. He had half a mind to cut in on the cozy couple.

Hey, slow down, that little voice warned him. *She's not marrying the guy—she's just dancing with him. What's it to you?*

Matt watched Derrick lean down and whisper something in her ear. As they turned to the music, he caught a glimpse of Ali's face as she looked up and laughed. You'd think the bum was a world-famous comedian, the way she's carrying on, Matt thought irritably.

"Are you having fun?"

Matt turned toward the feminine voice behind him. "Susan. Hank." Matt kissed Susan's proffered cheek, then shook Hank's hand and forced himself to exchange pleasantries with the couple, resisting the urge to turn around and keep an eye on the dance floor. He was relieved when the band struck up another tune and the newlyweds excused themselves. When he turned around, Ali and Derrick had vanished.

Matt edged his way to the foyer, where two bridesmaids were huddled in a conversation. They glanced up to give him coy smiles. Matt nodded abruptly and kept on moving, intent on avoiding being corralled into a conversation.

He re-entered the ballroom and worked his way around its perimeter, scanning the crowd. There was no sign of Ali or Derrick. An unaccustomed anxiety gripped him. Where the devil *were* they?

Matt was on his third lap around the room when he finally spotted Ali in the foyer. Thank goodness she was alone—but why was her face so flushed and pink? His suspicions made him clench his fists as he strode toward her.

"Matt! I'm glad you came." Ali smiled and started toward him, holding out both her hands.

Matt took them in his. Her fingers were like ice. "You're freezing," he observed.

"I was just outside with Derrick."

"I thought I told you to stay away from that worthless piece of trash," Matt said harshly, dropping her fingers.

The moment the words were uttered, he knew he'd overstepped his bounds. But it was too late; the statement lay between them like a gauntlet.

She arched her eyebrows. "And I thought I told *you* I don't need another big brother."

Matt couldn't suppress a scowl. "Looks to me like you do."

Ali didn't flinch. "You have no right to tell me what to do," she said, her eyes flashing with indignation.

Back off, Jordan. She's right. Matt drew a deep breath and struggled to regain his composure. He didn't want this to escalate into a scene. "Maybe not," he said, controlling his tone with an effort, "but I'd hate to see Robert's little sister get mixed up with a lowlife like that."

Ali placed her hands on her hips and fixed him with an exasperated glare. "I have half a mind to leave you to your sordid delusions," she said stiffly, "but the fact of the matter is that Derrick and the other groomsmen are decorating Hank's car. I went to show them where it was parked. Someone had already pulled it around front, so I came back in."

"Oh." Matt's immediate sense of relief was extinguished by the realization he'd just made a fool of himself for no reason. He seemed to have developed a habit of doing that every time he got anywhere near Ali, he realized with chagrin.

She was gazing up at him, her gray eyes bright and questioning. "What's going on here?"

Matt stared down at her. *I only wish I knew,* he thought.

"Come on, Matt," she prodded. "What's the story behind your obsession with Derrick?"

Matt shoved his hands into his pockets and shifted his stance. "I've already explained his reputation to you."

"I think there's something more personal to it." She eyed him challengingly for a moment. Matt's thoughts flipped back to the highly personal feelings he'd experienced in her bathroom that afternoon and he swallowed hard. He couldn't think of a coherent rebuttal to save his life.

But Ali was looking at him expectantly, waiting for a response. He cleared his throat and motioned to an upholstered bench along the foyer wall. She sat down and he lowered himself beside her.

"About a year ago, I ran into him at the Dew Drop Inn," Matt began.

Ali scrunched her face in an expression of distaste. "Isn't that the dive out on the highway?"

Matt nodded. "We'd just finished the framework on a custom home we were building for a rancher, and I wanted to treat the carpentry crew to a round of burgers and beers. It was the only place near the job site." Matt tried to find a more comfortable position on the narrow seat and ended up angling his knees toward her. "Derrick was playing pool with a bunch of oilfield roughnecks, and he was losing. He had a woman with him who was obviously crazy about him. And he, uh..." Matt found it difficult to continue.

"What?" Ali was staring at him in open curiosity. Matt hesitated, and she tugged on his arm. "What did he do, Matt? You can't start a story like this and then leave me hanging. It's not polite."

"Well, neither is the story." Matt gazed at the carpet. "Derrick offered her, um, *services* as ante in the game. He used very graphic terms—gave a personal endorsement. She left the bar in tears. I haven't been able to look at the man without wanting to deck him ever since." No point in telling her that's what he tried to do at the time—and would have, too, if his work crew hadn't restrained him.

Ali's hand flew to her mouth. "Oh, Matt. That's so... horrible."

"Yeah. It was." Matt looked at Ali. "So now you know. I just can't stomach the guy."

"Did you know the girl?"

"No," Matt said, "but it wouldn't have made any difference. No one deserves to be demeaned like that."

"What did you do?" Ali's eyes were locked on his face.

"I was going to offer her a ride, but I figured she wouldn't want to get in a car with a strange man who'd just heard Derrick's rude endorsement. So I paid one of the waitresses to take her home."

"That was kind of you," Ali said softly.

The praise rippled through him like fine scotch, spreading a feeling of warmth and ease throughout his chest. Matt realized his response was all out of proportion to her simple remark. He shrugged in what he hoped was a normal fashion. "Any decent guy would have done the same thing."

"No. Most people wouldn't have gotten involved in someone else's problems."

Ali's eyes were large and bright and admiring as she looked up at him. Her face was tilted at a kissable angle and her lips formed a soft, parted temptation.

What was he thinking? He was playing with fire. This was Robert's little sister, for heaven's sake—the scourge of calm and order and everything else he held dear.

Matt looked around, suddenly anxious for a way to end the discussion. He was no Fred Astaire, but the band was beginning a slow, familiar tune he thought he could handle. "Would you like to dance?" he asked.

"Sure."

Matt took her hand and led her into the ballroom. The moment he turned toward her, he realized the enormity of his mistake. The soft lighting on the dance floor made her lips even more inviting and cast enticing shadows between her breasts. He pulled her to him, irrationally thinking his heart would slow down if he held her so close he was unable to see her.

Wrong! He drew a deep breath to calm himself, and once again inhaled the soft, herbal scent of her hair. It had driven him wild earlier and it hadn't lost its impact.

Maybe if he turned his face away he wouldn't feel so intoxicated by it, he thought. He angled his head so that he rested his cheek against her temple.

But now he felt her breath on his neck. Prickles of pleasure ran down his spine, and he arched away from her so she wouldn't feel the effect she was having on him.

Dadblast it! How could dancing with a woman in a crowded room get him in such a state? The blood was pounding so loudly in his ears that it threatened to drown out the music. Matt was glad they were close enough to the bandstand that conversation was impossible; he doubted he could talk, even if he'd been able to think of anything to say.

Concentrate on moving your feet, he told himself. Focus on your extremities. He suddenly became overly aware of his hands. One rested low on her back, so low he could feel the beginning curve of her derriere beneath his fingers. He recalled the view of her backside that had resulted in his fall that morning. The thought made him miss a step, and Ali stepped on his toe.

"Sorry," she breathed. She adjusted her body against his, somehow managing to align herself in an even more provocative fashion.

Matt gritted his teeth. There are limits to what a man can take, he thought desperately. He had to move his hand; he was dying to crush her to him, and to do so in his present condition would only embarrass them both.

Matt drew his hand around to the side of her waist. Now he could feel the swell of her rib cage above it and the swell of her hip below it, and it only incited him more. He again wondered if he could span her waist with his hands, and experimentally splayed his fingers. He guessed that they reached almost halfway around her.

Oh, mercy. He didn't know where to put his hands, how to breathe, what to do with his feet—or how to control the adolescent response his body was having to this infuriating woman. He was trying to hold himself away from her, and he was developing a terrible crick in his back from the effort. With every passing second, he was in danger of losing his battle against nature. Every fiber of his being longed to pull her close, to breath her in, to taste her lips.

To make matters worse, she seemed completely oblivious to his struggle. She was snuggling against him as though dancing with him were the most natural, comfortable thing in the world. The longer they danced, the more relaxed she seemed to become. If the song went on much longer, she'd probably fall asleep!

When the *hell* was this infernal song going to end?

"Thank you," Ali said as the last notes of the melody faded. She pulled away from Matt's arms, feeling thoroughly shaken and a little unsteady on her feet. For a few minutes there, she could have sworn the room had disappeared and they'd drifted someplace else—someplace warm and dreamy and incredibly thrilling.

Oh, jeez, she thought despairingly. Why did she have to feel so attracted to Matt? She couldn't have developed a crush on a more unlikely prospect. He was one of the bossiest, most domineering men she'd ever met—exactly the type she considered pure poison. On top of that, he was Robert's handpicked selection—and her business partner to boot. A triple jeopardy selection!

Her feelings were just the result of the overly romantic atmosphere, she reassured herself. After all, what could be more sentimental than her best friend's wedding? Given a little time and distance, her feelings for Matt were sure to normalize.

Besides, the attraction seemed to be completely one-sided. Matt had been stiff and silent during the dance, and he'd resisted every one of her attempts to snuggle closer. Still, there had been a few moments when she'd sensed he might be interested. He'd rested his head against her hair for a few seconds and his hand had moved on her waist in a way that felt suspiciously like a caress.

"I'd better go find Susan," she said. "She'll need help changing from her wedding gown into her going away outfit."

She turned and fled the dance floor, grateful to have a duty to perform.

She found Susan already in the changing room, struggling with the tiny back buttons on her gown. A stab of guilt flashed through her; here she was, maid of honor at her best friend's wedding, and she'd gotten so absorbed in Matt that she'd forgotten her responsibilities. "Why didn't you come and get me?" Ali scolded gently. "I didn't know you were ready to change. Here, turn around and let me help."

"You looked like you were having too much fun on the dance floor," Susan said with a smile. "I didn't want to interrupt."

Ali quickly loosened the buttons and helped her friend step out of the gown, a flush heating her cheeks. Susan turned and eyed her closely. "Aha! I knew it." She wagged a finger at her. "Don't try and deny that you find Matt attractive. It's written all over your face."

Ali carefully placed the gown on its padded hanger. "Well, of course he's attractive," she said defensively. "Anyone can see that. But he's also impossibly overbearing. Would you believe he jumped my case about spending too much time with Derrick tonight?"

"Maybe he was jealous," Susan suggested.

"Fat chance! He thinks he's replaced Robert as my big brother."

Susan gave a sly grin. "He didn't look any too brotherly to me."

"I don't think you're in any position to make objective observations about these things," Ali retorted. "Those stars in your eyes are clouding your vision."

"You're probably right about that." A radiant smile lit Susan's face. "Oh, Ali, I'm so happy!" She twirled around, holding out her hand and admiring her wedding ring.

"No one deserves it more," Ali said warmly.

Susan gave her a quick hug, then reached for the clothes-hanger holding her new, pink wool suit. "I'd better hurry and get dressed. I don't want to keep my groom waiting—and I want to throw the bouquet before the guests start leaving." She gave Ali a stern look. "I fully expect you to catch it, you know."

Ali shook her head and laughed. "You don't give up, do you?"

They emerged five minutes later. Susan's mother bustled over and directed them to the dance floor, where the orchestra leader was announcing that the bride was about to throw her bouquet. Ali spotted Matt standing by the bandstand and was surprised at the surge of pleasure that shot through her. She'd halfway suspected he'd left after their dance.

Ali dutifully joined the throng of young women crowding to vie for the bouquet in front of the bandstand. Susan caught her eye and smiled.

The orchestra played a drum roll. Susan turned her back, drew back her arm and tossed.

Instead of heading toward the eager crowd of attendants waiting to catch it, the bouquet veered into the crowd of on-lookers and sailed directly at Matt. He flung up his hand to avoid being hit in the face and reflexively caught the bouquet.

Matt's first response was to glance at Ali to see if she were somehow responsible, but she looked as surprised as he felt. Matt suddenly realized the crowd was roaring with laughter, and decided his only course of action was to ham it up. He carried the bouquet through the crowd and presented it to Susan with a snappy salute.

"I believe you misfired, madam," he told her. The crowd laughed heartily.

The band began another drum roll and Susan tried again. This time the bouquet headed straight to Ali.

"Oh! Look who's going to be next!" someone shouted.

"Maybe this means she's going to marry the guy who caught it first," another voice said.

Matt watched a blush creep up Ali's cheeks as she found herself the center of attention. She was shy! The thought sur-

prised him. He'd figured her for the type who loved the lime-
light, but it evidently made her as uncomfortable as it did him.
The realization generated a protective urge in him and he began to head toward her. From all the things Robert had told
him about Ali, it had never occurred to Matt that she might be
bashful. It was beginning to look like there were a lot of things
about Ali that Robert had neglected to tell him.

Matt soon realized that the crowd was moving toward the
front door and Ali was being swept along with it. Hank and
Susan were evidently ready to leave.

Someone handed Matt a small packet of birdseed as he followed the herd outside. He found Ali on the outskirts of the
crowd and sidled up beside her. "Good catch," he remarked.

She returned his smile. "You, too. In fact, this belongs to
you." She held out the bouquet. "Since you caught it first,
looks like you'll be the next to walk the aisle."

Matt shook his head. "I'd rather walk the plank."

Ali looked up at him curiously. "What do you have against
marriage?"

Matt thrust a hand into his pocket, wishing he'd never
broached the subject. "It's not for me. I tried it once, and I
make a point of never making the same mistake twice."

"Once bitten, twice shy?"

"More like once nuked, twice determined to never let it
happen again."

Ali grinned. "I guess that means there's no special woman
in your life."

He shook his head, suddenly consumed with curiosity about
her own romantic status. He tried to adopt an offhanded
manner. "How about you? Did you leave someone special in
Dallas?"

"No."

He should have hoped she had a fiancé tucked away somewhere, that she'd come to Hillsboro after a lovers' spat and
would leave again as soon as they kissed and made up. If that
were the case, he wouldn't have to worry about keeping an eye
on her. But the truth was he'd held his breath until she'd answered and felt a deep wave of relief at her response.

He looked away to cover his confusion and was glad when she changed the subject.

"They did a pretty thorough job on the car, didn't they?"

Matt craned his neck and looked in the direction she pointed. The vehicle was so completely covered with shaving cream it was impossible to tell what color it was, much less its make and model. "It's probably the most thorough job Derrick ever did on anything in his entire life," Matt said wryly. "What a mess!"

"Here they come! Get your birdseed ready!" Ali yelled excitedly.

The newlyweds ran to the car, and Matt and Ali joined the crowd in pelting them with the seed. Hank struggled with the door on the passenger side as the seed storm continued.

"It looks like he's having trouble with his key," Ali commented.

"Maybe the shaving cream fouled up the lock," Matt said. "Look, they're going around to the other side."

With his arm protectively wrapped around Susan to shield her from the onslaught of birdseed, Hank tried the key on the driver's side. Still no luck.

The crowd ran out of birdseed and began offering advice.

"Are you sure you're using the right key?" someone called.

"Jiggle the handle!" recommended another.

Hank cleared a spot on the window with his hand and peered in the vehicle. "Hey!" he yelled. "This isn't my car!"

Matt threw back his head and whooped with laughter. "Derrick decorated the wrong car! Can you believe it? This is the one of funniest things I've ever seen!"

"But it's got to be his car! I pointed it out to Derrick myself!" Her forehead wrinkled in concern. "It's a blue Ford Taurus, and it's parked in the spot reserved for the groom's car."

A blue Ford Taurus? Matt turned to stare at the vehicle, taking in details that had escaped his notice earlier. Tin cans dangled from two long ropes tied to the rear bumper. Plastic streamers were attached to the windshield wipers and the rearview mirrors, and "Hot time tonight!" was written on the back window in what looked like chocolate syrup. The only part of the car that wasn't completely covered with foam was the license tag—and the numbers on it were naggingly familiar.

A sinking feeling hit the bottom of Matt's stomach. "Oh, no," he groaned. Ali had struck again.

"*There's* my car!" Hank announced, pointing to an automobile in the parking lot. He wrapped his arm around his bride and steered her toward it. "Thanks for the decoy, Derrick!" he called over his shoulder. "You saved us a stop at the car wash!"

Matt watched in dismay as the couple got in the vehicle and sped away, honking the horn at the well-wishers.

The crowd around them began filtering back into the building. Ali turned toward Matt, her face a study of confusion. "I don't understand. If Hank's car was still in the parking lot, whose car is that?" She pointed at the cream-covered vehicle.

A nerve twitched in Matt's jaw. "Whose car do you think it is?"

"I have no idea," Ali said.

"Let me give you a clue." Even to his own ears, his voice was clipped and tight. "Who has sustained a head injury, caught a somersaulting dog and a bridal bouquet, and been in a mind-spinning state of confusion ever since you hit town?"

Ali's hand flew to her mouth. Wide-eyed, she pointed back at the vehicle. "Yours?"

Matt nodded grimly.

"You have a blue Ford Taurus?"

Matt gave another reluctant nod. "Brand new. I've only had it three weeks."

"And you parked it right there?" she asked.

Dadblast it! She *would* have to point out that the incident was at least partially his fault.

Matt rubbed his chin and gave his head a rueful shake. "I should have known something was wrong. That parking space was too good to be true—and in my experience, when something seems too good to be true, it usually is."

"Oh, Matt. I'm so sorry." A smile ruffled the corners of her mouth.

Matt looked from her to the car and back again. He could tell she was trying hard not to laugh, but her eyes gleamed with amusement and her lower lip trembled with her effort to maintain a straight face. She broke into a grin and, despite his annoyance, Matt found himself returning it.

The next thing he knew, they were leaning against each other, laughing like tickled hyenas. They paused for breath, glanced at each other, and broke up all over again.

It felt great to cut loose like this, Matt thought with a little jolt of surprise. How long had it been since he'd laughed until his sides hurt? Too long. He'd been so busy working on the development, worrying about financing and generally being responsible that he hadn't made any time for fun.

He caught Ali's eye and burst into another round of laughter, putting an arm around her. She gave a little shiver and his arm tightened instinctively.

Was she trembling because she was cold or was she feeling the same surge of electricity, the one that was making him feel as though he'd touched a downed power line? He gazed into her eyes and her laughter abruptly ceased. Her lips parted and her breath came in fast little puffy clouds. His eyes riveted on her lips—lips so full and flushed and inviting that his head began lowering of its own volition.

The moment his mouth settled on hers, shock waves of pleasure pulsed through him. She moved her lips against his and reached her arms around his neck, pulling him down, and her responsiveness sent his temperature skyrocketing. He clutched her to him and deepened the kiss, laying siege to her lips like a man possessed.

What the hell was he doing? This was Robert's little sister, for heaven's sake. Any man worth his salt knew that you didn't fool around with your best friend's sister unless you were plenty serious about her, and he had no intention of getting serious about anyone, let alone a woman who would completely disrupt the calm, orderly life he'd built for himself.

He abruptly pulled back and dropped his arm from her shoulders. "Sorry," he muttered. "I don't know what happened. Must be the champagne." He'd had less than half a glass, but it was the only excuse that came to mind.

"Weddings make people sentimental," she mumbled.

"Yeah, that must be it." He grabbed at the explanation like a dog after a bone. "Well, you're freezing. Let's go inside." Taking her by the elbow, he headed toward the building.

Ali walked stiffly beside him, her arms folded across her chest. Tension hummed between them, mounting into an awkward silence. Anxious to diffuse it, Matt strove for a conversational tone. "Don't worry about the car. Anyone could have made the same mistake."

He held the door open for her and she brushed against him as she walked through it. A burst of adrenaline again shot through him at the contact, and he leaned away from her to minimize the effect. She turned toward him in the foyer. "The least I can do is give you a ride home. In the morning I'll bring you back and help you wash off your car."

She was standing close enough that Matt could again smell her intoxicating scent. He was tempted; he could invite her into his house for a drink, and then . . .

What on earth are you thinking, Jordan?

"I'd better get that goop off the car tonight or it'll ruin the paint job," Matt said curtly. "But thanks for the offer."

Ali brushed a stray curl from her forehead. "You'll have to clean off the windows to even drive it to a car wash. I'll go borrow some towels from the kitchen and meet you back outside."

She darted down the hall before he could object, her high heels clicking on the terrazzo. Matt jammed his hands in his pockets and walked back outside to survey the damage.

Ali joined him a few minutes later, bundled up in a black wool coat and a knit cap and carrying a stack of towels and a pitcher of water. The bottom of her pink gown peeked out below the coat, giving her a waiflike appearance. She looked flat-out adorable, a fact that bothered him to no end.

"Thanks," Matt said, taking the supplies from her and laying them on the ground. "I'll take it from here."

"But I feel responsible. I want to help," Ali protested.

"You've done quite enough already," Matt said. He wiped at the windshield with a towel. When he stepped back, shaving cream covered the front of his jacket and his slacks.

"Oh, dear," Ali moaned. She picked up a towel and began dabbing at his jacket, slipping a hand inside it to get a better grip on the material as she worked. Matt stood motionless as she rubbed his chest, barely able to breathe. Her soft, heady scent teased his nostrils.

Did she have any idea what she was doing to him? Didn't she realize he was a man? Despite the cold temperature, Matt began to break a sweat as she worked her way down his jacket. Heaven help him—was she going to try to clean his pants, too?

"Maybe you should just try pouring water on the windshield," she suggested.

Much more of this action and I'll need to pour it on myself.

Turning away abruptly, he picked the pitcher up off the ground and sloshed some water on the windshield, clearing a wide swath of glass.

"Thank goodness that worked," Ali said.

Matt raked a hand through his hair. "Thanks for the help. I'd better hurry if I want to find a car wash open." He took out his keys and unlocked the door.

"I'll come with you."

"No!" No telling what might happen if Ali got involved. Maybe the car wash would be out of water. Maybe the hose would spring a leak and he'd get completely drenched. Maybe dogs would somersault off the roof.

Or worse, maybe he'd give in to the urge he'd been fighting all evening and had already succumbed to once—to grab her in his arms and kiss her silly.

"It only takes one person to hold a water wand," Matt said in what he hoped was normal tone. "Thanks, but I can handle it." He got in the car and quickly closed the door, hoping the metal and glass would provide protection from his insane urges. Distance was the only sure cure. He suddenly felt the need to put quite a bit of it between them.

Ali waved as he sped away. The tin cans jingled and the streamers flapped as he drove out of the parking lot, but Ali felt none of her earlier amusement at the car's appearance. Instead, the sight caused an odd emptiness to tighten her chest.

Her fingers drifted to her lips where the imprint of Matt's mouth still burned. His kiss had affected her like nothing in her experience, sending her senses spinning until she was dizzy and dazed and confused. How could a simple thing like a kiss at a wedding make her feel like the world had suddenly careened off its axis?

Matt seemed to have recovered from it pretty quickly. In fact, he couldn't wait to get away from her. And who could blame him? He probably thought she was some sort of jinx. Once more she'd created a problem for him, when what she'd wanted to do was convince him she was capable and competent and . . . desirable.

Ali's heart skipped a beat at the admission. There was no denying a strong, instinctive pull toward Matt. Every time he'd touched her, her senses had buzzed and reeled, and when they'd laughed together, she'd felt the same sense of connectedness she'd experienced when they'd talked about Robert. She was certain he'd felt it, too.

But his practical nature had evidently overridden his sense of romance—which was just what she needed to do, too. After all, hadn't he pulled that insufferable bossy act on her again just this evening? Besides, he'd made it quite clear he had an aversion to involvement.

Ali sighed as she picked up the empty pitcher and the towels and headed back to the country club. No, a romantic relationship with Matt was totally out of the question. No matter how appealing he was, no matter how intrigued she might be with the idea that he had a gentle, caring side tucked away inside his armadillo-tough exterior, she had no business yearning for a romance with a man who exhibited all of the domineering, rigid, stuffed-shirt personality traits she'd vowed to avoid.

Besides, Matt was a business partner—and a reluctant one at that. Under the best of circumstances it was a mistake to mix business with pleasure, and in this situation, it would no doubt be disastrous.

She needed to take a businesslike approach to her relationship with Matt, and she intended to do just that. She couldn't let anything compromise her goal. After all, working on Robert's designs wasn't just a job to her; it was her chance to take care of the big brother who had so often taken care of her. It was a final act of love—and in a way, it was her declaration of independence.

Ali dropped off the towels and headed back outside to her car, lifting her chin in resolve. From now on, she'd show Matt Jordan nothing but logic and reason and order. She'd just forget how she'd melted in his arms on the dance floor. She wouldn't notice how the corners of his eyes formed those devastatingly attractive wrinkles when he smiled. And she wouldn't think about how he'd forever changed her perception of what a kiss could be.

Chapter Six

Ali paused outside the double mahogany doors and eyed the engraved brass sign. Cimarron Homebuilders. This was it, all right. Even without the sign, she would have guessed that this was the right place. The thick Georgian columns on the two-story brick structure reminded her of her brother's fondness for neoclassic architecture.

But the building was much more impressive than she'd imagined. Intimidating, almost.

Like Matt.

Ali squared her shoulders at the thought. She was here to claim her rightful place in the company and nothing—Matt Jordan included—was going to stop her. She straightened the jacket of her red wool suit, shifted her black leather briefcase to her other hand and pushed her way through the doorway.

The exterior looked like Robert, but the interior was pure Matt—modern, masculine, clean-lined. It was surprising how well the two different styles blended together. Much like the two men's personalities must have blended in their business, Ali thought as she crossed a brick foyer to a thickly carpeted reception area.

She stopped in front of a massive desk and addressed a middle-aged woman seated behind it. "I'd like to see Matt Jordan, please."

The woman regarded her with friendly curiosity. "I'm afraid Mr. Jordan is tied up in a meeting. Is there something I can help you with, Miss, er . . ."

"McAlester," Ali supplied.

"Robert's sister?" The woman smiled broadly and rose from her chair, extending both of her hands toward Ali as she circled the desk. "But of course. I recognize you from the pictures he used to keep in his office. I thought you looked familiar the moment you walked in. It's a pleasure to finally meet you!"

Ali took her hands and grinned. "Thank you. You must be Hattie."

The woman nodded. "None other."

"Robert spoke of you often. He was very fond of you."

Hattie's brown eyes grew moist behind her bifocals. "It was mutual. He and Matt were like sons to me." A single tear escaped from her full eyes. "I want to apologize for not attending the funeral. I didn't dare go for fear I'd make a spectacle of myself."

Hattie's tears touched Ali's heart and made her feel perilously close to crying herself. She swallowed hard and impulsively put her arm around the diminutive woman, giving her a little hug. "I don't blame you at all," she said softly. "The truth is I was such a mess myself I wouldn't have known if you were there or not."

Hattie nodded and clutched Ali's free hand. Ali patted her shoulder, and the two women shared a moment of empathetic silence. By the time Hattie pulled away, Ali knew she'd found a new friend.

"Can I get you anything?" Hattie asked. "Coffee? A cola?"

"No, thank you. But I'll tell you what I would like. Do you think I could wait for Matt in Robert's old office?"

"Certainly." Hattie smiled. "I'll show you where it is."

Ali followed her down the carpeted hallway to a door with a brass plate that read Robert H. McAlester.

Ali reached up and ran a finger over the name. A wave of grief rolled through her, grief sharpened by a sense of injustice. Robert should be on the other side of the door, doing the work he loved. It wasn't fair that he wasn't, that he never would again. It wasn't fair that a drunk driver should be alive and her talented brother's life should be over.

Hattie eyed her sympathetically. "I know just how you feel," she said gently. "Every time I see his name up there I get weepy, too."

Ali gave Hattie a tremulous smile, drew a steadying breath and opened the door. She stepped into the large office and gazed around, taking in the unadorned walls, the bare oak desk and the empty bookshelves in the corner. She turned quizzically to Hattie. "All of Robert's things are gone."

"Matt boxed them up and took them to your house," Hattie explained.

Ali paused, remembering the drafting tools. "That explains the box in the garage."

Hattie nodded sympathetically. "Matt thought cleaning out Robert's office might be hard on you. He's the one who handled everything at the house, you know."

Ali stared at her in surprise. "I thought the attorneys hired someone."

Hattie shook her head. "It was Matt."

The information rattled Ali. She vaguely remembered someone at the funeral asking if she wanted help sorting through Robert's belongings and closing up the house. She'd thought it was a representative from her attorney's office and had responded that she couldn't bear to even think about it.

But it had been Matt. At the time, she'd been in such a fog of grief and shock that it hadn't registered.

Ali turned to the window as the extent of the details Matt had handled began to sink in. He would have had to deal with everything from stopping the mail to disposing of the food in the kitchen. He must have boxed up Robert's clothes and toiletries, canceled the phone service and performed innumera-

ble other painful chores. Ali knew how hard it was to sort
through the remains of a life; she'd done it when her mother
had died, and she'd felt as though she couldn't go through it
again after Robert's accident.

But it couldn't have been easy for Matt, either, Ali reflected. The two men had been the closest of friends. A lump
formed in Ali's throat. Matt had spared her a tremendous
amount of grief and hadn't even told her about it.

"Are you all right?" Hattie asked, her brow creased with
concern.

Ali realized she was still staring out the window, sightlessly
gazing at the wind-tossed oak trees on the empty lot across the
street. She turned to face the older woman. "I'm fine."

Hattie hesitated, her hand on the door. "Well, I'll let Matt
know you're here as soon as his meeting breaks up," she said.
"Are you sure I can't bring you anything?"

"I'm sure. Thank you."

Alone in the room, Ali walked to the desk and tentatively
lowered herself into the chair. Matt was a complex man, she
mused. Robert had described him as structured and methodi-
cal, and she knew from personal experience that he could be
maddeningly domineering. But she'd discovered at Susan's
wedding that he also had an unexpected sense of humor. And
the sensuous, passionate nature he'd revealed when he'd kissed
her had shocked her to the core.

This new information, however, was even more disturbing
than that mind-numbing kiss, and it elevated her attraction to
him to a whole other plane. It revealed a deeply kind and
thoughtful side, and in her opinion, nothing made a man sex-
ier than being kind and thoughtful.

Ali spun around in the swivel chair, trying to spin the idea
out of her head, and deliberately directed her thoughts along
a less dangerous path.

Business. Keep your mind on business.

Well, she could only hope Matt would apply some of his
kind, thoughtful nature to her business proposition. Perhaps
he would be more receptive now that he'd had a chance to get

used to the idea. She certainly hoped so—especially in view of the drastic action she'd taken this morning.

Chances were it would make him angry. After all, Matt thought she'd given up on her plan to play an active role in the company. Ali worried her bottom lip, her stomach tightening at the thought of a confrontation with Matt.

Face it—the thought of any encounter with Matt makes you uneasy. The reason wasn't a lack of confidence in her ability to hold her own when it came to business. What had her worried was the distressing way he affected her physically.

Ali leaned back in the chair and absently fingered the armrests. She'd dated her share of men in her twenty-five years, but she'd never experienced anything like the knee-weakening giddiness she'd felt when Matt took her in his arms. How was she supposed to hold her own against *that?*

Abruptly, she pushed out of the chair and headed to the window. Staring out, she gave herself a silent pep talk. Okay, so she was attracted to Matt. So what? It didn't mean she was going to act on it. Lots of people experienced attractions they never did anything about. In any case, her plans were too important to allow for any distractions. Matt was her business partner—even if he didn't know it yet—and she intended to limit her involvement with him to working on the Victorian Village.

Deliberately turning her thoughts in that direction, Ali strode to the drafting table and opened a set of neatly bound blueprints that lay on top of it. Paydirt! They were the plans for Robert's homes. Ali pulled up a chair and determinedly settled down to study them.

By the time the door opened twenty minutes later, she was completely engrossed.

"Ali! What a surprise."

Ali jumped at Matt's voice and jerked her head toward the doorway. Despite her earlier resolution, her heart pounded at the sight of him.

"I suppose you came for the grand tour. Let me show you around."

It wasn't why she'd come, but it was probably a good idea, Ali decided. She was curious about the business facilities. Besides, a tour would buy her time to calm herself before she brought up a topic he was sure to find unpleasant. "I'd love to see the place," she replied.

Matt held the door. Her arm accidently brushed his rock-hard chest as she walked by and a hot tingle singed its way to her shoulder. "Excuse me," she murmured.

"Sorry," he said simultaneously.

She quickly moved away, but not before she'd inhaled his clean, masculine scent. Ali's palms grew damp. *I need to find out what shaving cream he uses and start applying it to Flipper,* she thought as she followed Matt down the hall. *If I start associating that scent with a dog, maybe I won't have this reaction to it.*

Matt drew a ragged breath and opened a heavy door, careful to back away as Ali stepped up to peer in. He didn't want to risk any further contact with her; his chest still felt the imprint of her touch and his pulse revved like a race car.

"This is the conference room."

"Is this where you meet with clients?"

He glanced down at her and found her appearance so distracting he could hardly follow the conversation. She was drop-dead gorgeous in that red suit, and she seemed oblivious to the fact. She brushed a wisp of hair from her forehead and he followed the motion of her fingers, mesmerized. Her thick chestnut mane was pulled back from her face with combs, but little strands escaped at her temples and ears, softly framing her face.

He found himself wondering if the springy curls felt as soft as they looked. He'd like to find out; he'd love to plunge his fingers into her heavy, herbal-scented tresses, tilt back her head and find out if her lips were really as luscious as the memory that had plagued him all weekend.

What's gotten into you, Jordan? If you're going to fantasize about Ali, you might as well fantasize about being in traction, because that's where you're likely to end up.

She was looking at him expectantly, and Matt realized she was still waiting for an answer to her question about the conference room.

"We use this for all kinds of meetings," he responded curtly, snapping off the light and ushering her down the hallway.

Matt had intended to give her a cursory tour and send her on her way as soon as possible, but Ali peppered him with questions as he guided her through the building. To his surprise, he found he enjoyed answering them. The business was his favorite topic and he'd never had a more raptly attentive audience. It was only natural she'd be interested in her late brother's business, he reasoned.

"I'm impressed," Ali said sincerely as they completed their rounds of the building. "I had no idea your operation was this large."

He was impressed, too. Her questions were perceptive and indicated she had a surprisingly good grasp of the basics of home building.

In spite of his earlier misgivings, Matt felt his chest swell with pride. "Would you like to see the equipment yard?" he asked impulsively.

"Sure."

Once outside, Matt noticed that several of the men stopped their work to eye Ali appreciatively. He followed their gaze to her legs as a gust of wind blew up her hem to reveal a lacy black slip and a provocative length of slender thigh. His mind shifted to the undergarment he'd glimpsed in her kitchen, and he couldn't help but wonder what else she was or wasn't wearing under her businesslike suit.

The thought made his mouth run dry. Another gust caught her skirt from the other side and he swallowed hard. She was studying the equipment, completely unaware of the effect she was having on him or the other men around her.

It was one thing for him to admire her assets, and quite another for anyone else to get an eyeful. He was vaguely aware that his logic was flawed but decided to act on it anyway.

"It's too cold to stay out here," Matt said abruptly. He placed a hand on her arm and led her back inside, steering her to his office.

Ali looked around as she seated herself on a burgundy chair opposite Matt's desk. The floorplan was the same as Robert's office and the furnishings were identical, but there the similarity ended. A neat stack of messages sat by Matt's phone, his In box was filled with a carefully aligned pile of papers awaiting his attention and the top of his credenza held an array of color-coded files stacked with geometric precision. He was even more meticulous than she'd imagined.

"That's pretty much the whole operation," Matt said, leaning back in his chair. "Is there anything else I can do for you today?"

Ali nervously cleared her throat, then drew a deep breath. He'd taken more than an hour to courteously show her around, but he was obviously anxious to get back to work. It was time to address the real reason behind her visit. "I hate to take up any more of your time, but there's something I need to discuss with you," she told him.

An eyebrow rose quizzically on his chiseled face. "Yes?"

Ali twisted her fingers together in her lap. "I went to see Arnold Armstrong this morning."

His other eyebrow jerked upward in surprise. "The loan officer at the bank?"

She nodded, and his brow crinkled in concern. He leaned across his desk. "Ali, if you need anything, I'll be happy to help. I would have offered earlier, but I thought Robert's life insurance policy would keep you well fixed for a while—at least until I can buy out Robert's half of the company. You know all of the business assets are stretched to the limit because of the development, but I could make you a personal loan . . ."

She quickly shook her head, twisting her fingers in her lap. The fact he was being so kind didn't make her feel any better. The minute she mentioned what she'd done, he'd hit the roof. "No, I don't need anything personally. I went to see Mr. Armstrong about a business loan."

Matt leaned back in the chair, resting an elbow on each upholstered leather arm and making a triangle with his fingertips. His face registered surprise, but showed no sign of wariness. "Are you planning to open your own business, Ali?"

Ali squirmed uneasily. "Not exactly. At least, not just yet."

"A partnership? Perhaps you and Susan are looking to open a decorating business?"

It irritated her that he was so completely certain she'd abandoned her idea of playing an active role in the company. Did he really think she'd give up so easily?

She decided to string him along. "It's a partnership, but not with Susan."

"Then who's the lucky person?"

Ali couldn't resist a wicked grin. "You are."

For a moment she thought he would topple over in his chair. His eyes narrowed and a muscle twitched in his jaw. He leaned across his desk, his displeasure a palpable thing, and Ali's pulse quickened.

"Now, Ali, we've already discussed this," he began sternly. "I've explained that I have no intention of incurring any more indebtedness on his project."

"You're not incurring any more indebtedness. I am."

"Perhaps you'd better explain just what the hell you've gone and done," Matt said, his voice a low growl.

"I mortgaged the house." She opened her briefcase, pulled out the papers and handed them to him across the polished desk. Settling back in her chair, she watched his face blanch as he read the amount.

His brow creased into a frown and his mouth tensed into a hard line. "What the hell is this all about, Ali?" he demanded.

She tried to keep her voice calm even though her heart was pounding erratically. "This is about decorating the interiors of the Victorian Village homes."

Matt's scowl deepened.

Ali leaned forward, placing her hands on the edge of his desk. *I've got to make him understand,* she thought earnestly. "I want to make these homes a showcase, Matt. I want Robert's architectural talent to get the recognition it deserves. I want this development to be a tremendous success."

"And you don't think I'm capable of managing that?" The words were clipped and tight.

"I didn't say that."

"You didn't need to. The implication was clear enough." Matt rose from his chair as if to indicate the conversation was over.

Ali remained seated. She clasped her hands together to hide the fact that they were shaking and crossed her legs in an effort to appear collected. "Matt, that's not at all what I meant. I have every confidence that you'll make the village a financial success."

Matt loomed over her, his face as dark as a summer thundercloud. "So what's the issue here? Exactly what *are* you trying to say?"

Ali forced herself to sit calmly and look him in the eye, although her muscles were taut with the urge to flee the room. "I'm simply saying that in order to be true to the architectural concept, the interiors should have some Victorian charm."

"Robert didn't put anything about 'charm' in his plans."

"Of course not. I'm talking about interior design elements—paint, wallpaper, flooring, light fixtures—not architectural elements."

They locked eyes in a standoff.

"And just how do you plan to recoup your investment?" Matt demanded. "I suppose you expect me to agree to raise the cost of the homes enough to cover your extravagances?"

Ali felt the color rise in her face along with her temper. "These 'extravagances,' as you call them, will raise the value of the homes." She pulled the file from her briefcase and laid it smartly on his desk. "These statistics prove that consumers are willing to pay more to get the items that make a house really special, that give it character."

Matt dismissed her remark with a wave of his hand. "Homes with character take longer to sell," he said. "Not every home buyer wants powder blue carpet or chartreuse walls or whatever the heck it is you're itching to do to these houses. Once you get away from neutral shades, you're in danger of alienating a potential buyer. Then there's another little fact you haven't taken into account. In Hillsboro, the higher the cost of a house, the longer it usually takes to sell it. We're so heavily financed that we don't have all the time in the world to sell these homes. The interest alone could eat up our profit margin in a shockingly short period of time."

Matt turned away from her and strode to the window. His broad back formed an intimidating spectacle. Ali stared at it, paralyzed by a sharp pang of doubt. Robert had been the architect, but Matt had handled all of the business decisions. He obviously knew what he was doing or the company wouldn't have prospered—and the bank would never have loaned him the money to build the development.

How could she presume to tell him what would sell in this market and what wouldn't, or what people would be willing to pay? All she had was a knack for making houses into homes and a gut feeling that this would work.

Well, she might not be an expert, but she was sure of one thing. "All I know is that Robert's designs deserve more than white walls and tan carpet," she said in a quiet voice. "I feel obligated to do everything I can to see that his final project is everything he intended."

Matt turned slightly. Not enough to face her directly, just enough to reveal his profile—enough to indicate he was listening.

Ali screwed up her courage and continued. "And I can't help but believe that distinctive interiors could be a real asset if they're marketed properly. I have a lot of ideas along those lines. Furnished homes have a lot more appeal than empty buildings, and—"

Matt held up a hand. "Whoa. Furnished homes?"

Ali nodded. "I want to work with local fabric stores and furniture shops and antique dealers to furnish a few of the homes for a Designer's Showcase. I've spoken to the life-styles editor at the local newspaper and she said they'd love to feature it. The stores would welcome the opportunity to showcase their furnishings and get publicity. It would be a great way to attract potential home buyers."

Matt met her gaze, his eyes guarded but thoughtful. Ali folded her fingers tightly together in her lap and decided the time had come to divulge the larger part of her dream. "There's another thing. I've already talked to the editor of *American Homelife* magazine. She said they'd be interested in doing a feature on a couple of the houses if they were strikingly decorated." Ali gripped the arms of her chair and leaned forward. "Don't you see, Matt? It would be a way for Robert's designs to get the recognition they deserve. Maybe we could even sell the blueprints and his homes could be built throughout the country."

Matt turned toward her and studied her intently for a long moment. She forced herself to sit still, clenching her fingers so tightly that her nails dug into her palms. She didn't realize she'd been holding her breath until she saw his mouth softened from its tight set.

"It would be great to see Robert's work recognized outside of Hillsboro," he finally said. He turned and stood behind his chair, thoughtfully drumming his fingers on its tall leather back. "I have to admit that what you say makes some sense."

A burst of elation surged through Ali's veins. Her excitement was cut short when Matt raised a cautioning hand. "But there's another issue here." He rubbed his jaw and eyed her questioningly. "I don't know how to put this politely, so I'll just get to the point. Quite frankly, I have no way of knowing if you're any good at what you do."

The comment stung, even as she acknowledged its truth. After all, he'd never seen her work. It was irrational to want him to believe in her abilities without proof. And yet part of her wanted just that.

It was important that she respond like a professional. "I can give you references," she offered. "The firm I worked for in Dallas and any of my former clients will be happy to vouch for me."

Matt reseated himself behind his desk and leaned back in the chair. Her references would only tell him how well she could adapt to someone else's tastes, he thought, not how she'd handle a project on her own. The question was whether he was willing to take a risk or not. He rested an ankle on his knee and studied her as he pondered the situation.

She was sitting ramrod straight in her chair and looking at him as if he held the key to her future. In a way, he guessed he did. If there were a market for Robert's designs beyond the housing development he was constructing, it would provide her with an additional source of income. And there was another angle to this that she hadn't mentioned: if she succeeded with this project, she'd be able to write her own ticket professionally.

This project meant a lot to her, he thought. After all, she'd quit her job, made a move and mortgaged her home. She was obviously committed to it.

Then there was the fact that she was Robert's sister. Matt sighed deeply, knowing that there was no way he could deny her this opportunity despite all of his misgivings. Especially when she was looking at him like that with those enormous blue-gray eyes.

She'll drive you crazy. She'll spend extra money you don't need to spend. She'll jinx the project. Worst of all, she'll make you want her to the point of distraction.

Matt drummed his fingers on his desk and silently swore.

She was Robert's sister, and he simply had no choice. Matt leaned forward over the desk. "Okay. You can tackle two houses."

Ali's face lit up like the sky on the fourth of July. "Make it four and you've got a deal," she countered.

"Three," Matt said. His voice brooked no room for further negotiation, but he secretly admired her spunk. "The homes are being constructed in groups of three. You can take the first group and we'll see what happens."

"Will I get to do the others if I'm successful?"

"Let's start with the first three and see how it goes," Matt said gruffly. "And there are a few conditions you'll have to agree to. I want to approve everything before it's installed, and I reserve the right to veto anything I think is too farfetched or out of line. And we're going to set a limit on what you spend on each house.''

Ali's grin spread from ear to ear. "That sounds reasonable.''

"One more thing," Matt warned. "The interiors have to be completed according to our original time schedule. We're going to have a hard enough time dealing with weather delays this time of year, and I won't tolerate any additional holdups.''

"You won't have to," she reassured him.

"I hope you understand that this is just a temporary arrangement," Matt cautioned. "After these homes are sold, I want to follow my initial plan and buy out your shares of the company.''

"You don't have to worry. I'm not going to foist myself on you as a permanent partner." Her grin was so wide, her face so aglow with excitement, that Matt felt a touch of it himself. He was surprised to discover he was smiling.

"You'll need a place to work. I'll have Hattie help you get settled in Robert's old office," he found himself saying.

"Great," Ali said.

What are you doing? If you have any sense, you'll get her out of here before you give away the store.

He pushed himself out of his chair. "Anything else you need?''

Ali unfolded her legs, and Matt found himself mesmerized by the motion. His eyes traveled the smooth length from her suede pumps to the hem of her short red skirt and back again. He swallowed hard and ran a finger under his collar. She had the best set of legs since Betty Grable.

Ali stood and picked up her briefcase. "I'd like to see the construction site," she replied.

Matt pulled his eyes from her legs with an effort. "I'm going out there this afternoon around four. You're welcome to come with me.''

Thinking about the job site made him knit his brows into a frown. With her dangling earrings, short skirt and impractical shoes, she would be a workplace hazard—not to mention a serious distraction for his construction workers. "You'd better change clothes before we go. High heels and mud don't mix,'' he said gruffly.

Second thoughts weighed on his mind as he crossed the room to escort her out the door. Oh, Lord, what had he done? He'd probably just made the worst move of his career. He'd broken his own cardinal rule and based a business decision purely on sentiment. Surely there were other ways he could help her achieve the same goals. If he thought fast, maybe he could still rectify the situation.

"Look, Ali . . ." he began.

She turned toward him, her eyes luminous and wide with gratitude. "Thanks, Matt," she said softly. "You won't be sorry about this."

She held out her hand, and Matt folded it in his own. It felt so soft and fragile in his palm that he gave it a gentle squeeze instead of the businesslike shake he'd intended. He took another look at her beaming face and knew there was no way he could back out of the deal. He gave her the closest thing to a smile he could manage and closed the door behind her.

Alone again in his office, Matt sighed heavily and turned toward the window, raking his fingers through his hair. "Now I know what the term 'temporary insanity' means," he muttered, resting a hand on the window frame.

Had he really agreed to let Tornado Ali rip through three of his houses and do heaven only knew what to the interior? What had he been thinking, offering her an office in his building? And why had he made arrangements to take her with him this afternoon when he had serious business to conduct with the framing carpenter?

He just wasn't himself around her. She made him feel confused and befuddled and out of control. And here he'd gone and agreed to an arrangement that guaranteed he was going to feel that way every day until the development was finished.

Matt strode to his desk and lowered himself into his deep leather chair. No telling what kind of havoc she was likely to wreak in his nice, orderly life—a life he'd carefully constructed, a life that was largely predictable and devoid of surprises, a life he tightly controlled and liked just fine the way it was.

He rested his elbows on the gleaming mahogany desk and sank his face in his hands. "Won't be sorry?" he moaned. "I already am."

Hattie poked her head inside Matt's office later that afternoon. "Ali said to tell you she's ready to go when you are," she announced. "She's in her office."

Matt looked up from the paperwork in front of him. The thought of Ali two doors down the hall in "her" office made his head begin to throb.

The receptionist grinned at him. "I think it's wonderful that she's going to be working here. Those houses need a woman's touch—and so do you, if you don't mind my saying so."

Matt rubbed his temples. "It just so happens I do mind, Hattie," he grumbled.

The older woman shook her head and clucked disapprovingly. "See what I mean? You're grumpy as an old bear with an empty honey jar. You need someone to sweeten you up." A gleam lit Hattie's eyes as she picked up a stack of papers to be typed and filed from a leather tray on his desk. "Ali's awfully pretty, isn't she? And she's just as nice as she is lovely. Reminds me a lot of Robert. Yes, sir, you could do a lot worse."

"This happens to be a business, not a lonely hearts club," Matt groused. "No one around here seems to remember we're trying to turn a profit. Ali thinks Cimarron Homebuilders is some sort of negative cashflow experiment."

"I think that girl's going to surprise you," Hattie said confidently.

"No doubt. Why do you think I'm so worried?"

Hattie harrumphed her way out of the room wearing a knowing smile.

Matt closed the file he'd been studying and placed it in a stack of papers to be dealt with later. He'd never admit it to Hattie, but he'd been unable to get Ali off his mind ever since her morning visit. Despite his best efforts to concentrate on work, he kept seeing her bright eyes, her unruly mane of hair, her tempting, bee-stung lips. And the memory of those long legs of hers made it darn near impossible to focus on the construction estimates he'd been trying to review all afternoon.

Matt frowned and pushed back his chair. He should be worrying about her impact on his business, not his libido.

Well, he only had to put up with her for a couple of months. Surely he could handle that. Just two short months, then life would be back to normal.

Cheered by the thought, Matt grabbed his coat and headed down the hall. He pulled up short when he saw one of his carpenters fiddling with the door to her office.

"What are you doing?" Matt asked.

The man pointed a screwdriver at Robert's nameplate, which dangled by a single screw. "Takin' this off for the little lady."

Matt stared at the wobbling nameplate and clenched his jaw. He wasn't ready to have it removed. No one could ever replace his close friend and partner, and seeing the empty screw holes in the door would only remind him of his loss.

Maybe Ali intended to put her name on the door. Tension coiled through his neck. How dare she make a decision like this without consulting him—especially since he'd made it clear that their partnership was temporary? Who did she think she was?

Your new business partner, he reminded himself grimly, *whether you like it or not.*

Still, there was something high-handed about the move that struck a nerve. He brushed past the carpenter and entered the office.

The nameplate wasn't the only change, he realized as he stood in the middle of the room and looked around. She'd wasted no time putting her imprint on the place. She'd already rearranged the furniture and from the number of plants strewn about the office, it looked like she'd bought out the local nursery. He spotted Ali in the corner behind a ficus tree, half hidden by its leaves as she tugged it into position.

Play it cool, he warned himself.

"What's going on here?" he asked as casually as he could manage.

She looked up and smiled. "Just settling in."

"I see you couldn't wait to get your own name on the door," he commented.

Ali straightened, wiped her hands on her jeans and regarded him quizzically. Matt thrust his hands into his pockets and tried to look nonchalant, but he had the uneasy feeling that she saw right through his act. "I'm not interested in having a nameplate," she said quietly. "I just don't want to feel sad every time I walk through the door. Seeing Robert's name up there was pretty hard to take. I hope you don't mind. I thought I'd put up a doorknocker to hide the screw holes."

Matt guiltily diverted his gaze to the floor. Nothing she'd ever done or said gave him cause to think she was into self-aggrandizement, and he knew she missed Robert as much as he did. Maybe more; she was Robert's sister, for heaven's sake. Instead of looking for ways to help her, as he'd originally planned, he was looking for reasons to dislike her. Matt shifted uneasily. *Give her a break,* he told himself.

"Actually, I've been meaning to take it down myself," he admitted. "I just never could quite bring myself to do it."

Ali gave him an empathetic smile. "I know how that is," she said softly. "I felt the same way about making any changes at the house, even though the place reminds me so strongly of Robert I practically feel like crying every time I walk through the door. Then it dawned on me that Robert never knowingly made me sad when he was alive, and he wouldn't want to do it now."

Matt regarded her with interest. "So what are you planning to do?"

"Redecorate. Re-paint and paper the walls, reupholster the living room furniture, hang some new window treatments."

What the heck was a "window treatment"? The windows were fine as far as he could tell. "I don't know who does upholstery work, but I'll give you the names of the paint and wallpaper subcontractors we use," Matt offered. "I'm sure they'll give you a break on the cost."

Ali smiled. "Thanks. I'll need their names for the work on the spec houses, but I plan to do the work at home myself."

Matt looked at her incredulously. "You're going to do all that yourself?"

"Sure." She gave him a teasing grin. "Although I'm accepting weekend volunteers. Care to enlist?"

Matt raked a hand through his hair. It was no doubt the sort of thing Robert would have done for his sister, and his original intention had been to look out for her like a brother. Besides, Matt's conscience burned over the way he'd practically accused her of being eager to get her name on the door. What the heck, he thought. It wouldn't hurt him to play good Samaritan for a couple of weekends.

"I'll help—but only if you lock up Flapper. I don't want to be climbing any ladders with your kamikaze stunt dog around."

"His name is Flipper," Ali corrected with a grin. "And I promise to keep him outside whenever a ladder is involved. Thanks, Matt."

Matt shrugged, suddenly self-conscious under her brilliant smile. "Don't mention it," he said.

Her expression suddenly turned serious. "There's something else I haven't thanked you for—taking care of the house and sorting through Robert's belongings after the accident. It was a huge job and I know it must have been painful for you." Her eyes were soft and warm, and they melted something inside him. "I don't know why, but I didn't realize you'd handled it until I talked to Hattie today. I guess I just assumed the attorneys for the estate had taken care of it. Anyway, I want you to know that you saved me a lot of grief. I—I can't tell you how much I appreciate it."

The way her eyes misted over made a lump form in his throat. "Hey, I was glad to help."

They stood regarding each other as emotion crackled between them. If she'd been anybody else, he probably would have reached out and hugged her, but he didn't trust himself to touch her. There was something between them—something that thickened the air and made it hard to breathe, something that made casual contact impossible.

With an effort, he cleared his throat. "I'm supposed to meet the framing contractor at the job site, so we'd better get a move on."

Maybe fresh air would clear his thinking. He sure hoped something would.

Chapter Seven

"Here we are," Matt said, steering the company pickup onto an unpaved road.

Ali braced her hand on the dashboard as the truck bounced over the rough dirt, deliberately leaning toward the door to avoid being thrown against Matt.

Thank goodness the ride was almost over; the pickup cab was entirely too small and intimate for comfort. Or maybe Matt was just too large and disturbing. Either way, being confined in such close proximity to him made her edgy as a cat on a ledge.

Clutching her hands together in her lap, Ali angled her shoulder away from him and gazed out the windshield at the hillside. The beginnings of spring were sprouting in the wintery landscape. Oak, redbud and persimmon trees covered the rolling hills in varied shades of tender green.

"Oh, Matt, it's beautiful here," she breathed.

Matt tossed her a sideways grin as he steered the truck around a particularly deep rut. "I hope twenty qualified homebuyers agree with you. See those stakes?" He pointed to a line of orange sticks set at regular intervals among the trees.

Ali nodded. "What are they?"

"Markers for the lots."

"They look large," Ali remarked.

"About an acre each," Matt affirmed. "We made them large to help preserve the natural beauty of the area. We're working carefully to preserve as many trees as possible, too." He shifted gears as the truck climbed a hill. "Robert and I gambled that the location was pretty enough that people wouldn't mind the ten-minute drive to town."

"I bet you're right," Ali said. "I know I wouldn't mind it at all."

Matt pulled the pickup to the side of the road behind a red flatbed truck and turned off the engine. Ali's eyes followed his hands as he removed the key from the ignition.

During the brief drive from the office, she'd found herself frequently watching his hands, aware of how his fingers rested lightly on the steering wheel, how they shifted gears with easy strength. His hands were strong, tanned and covered with a sprinkling of dark masculine hair, and she found them objects of fascination. They were the hands of a man accustomed to using them and they set her imagination to racing.

The truth was that just about every part of the man was fantasy material, Ali thought ruefully. To keep her mind from wandering into dangerous territory, she'd kept up a steady stream of questions about the development during the ride.

"There's the first house," Matt said, nodding toward a wooden skeleton of a home set back in the trees. "If you had a chance to look at the plans, you'll recognize it as the one with the wraparound porch."

Ali anxiously peered out the passenger door window, glad to have something to focus on besides Matt's masculine attributes. "Oh, that's my favorite!" she exclaimed. "Look— you can see the outline of the round turret at the corner."

Matt rested his arm on the back of the seat and leaned toward her as he looked out at the structure, his eyes intent and glowing. "Sure can," he said. "Looks like they got most of the framing up today." His voice held a note of satisfaction that made her glance up at him. Pleasure played across the strong planes of his face and radiated from his light brown eyes as he regarded the house.

This development means as much to him as it does to me, Ali thought with surprise. *He really loves his work.* Somehow, she'd never thought of Matt in those terms. He'd been the practical one, the workhorse, the one who made Robert's exciting designs become reality. It hadn't dawned on her that he would get as much satisfaction from his end of the business as Robert had from his.

"Let's go have a look," he said, opening his door.

Ali reached for the door handle on the passenger side. Matt shot her a staying glance. "I'll come around and get the door for you," he instructed. "Just stay put."

Ali hesitated, appreciating the masculine courtesy but feeling silly just sitting there while he circled the truck. She'd compromise, she decided. She'd open the door, but let him help her down.

The door stuck slightly. Ali threw her full weight against it— just as Matt came alongside.

"Ooomph!" he gasped. The force of it sent him careening down the drainage ditch that ran beside the road.

"Oh, no!" Ali moaned, flinging herself out of the truck after him.

The ground sloped away sharply under her feet. She found herself staggering down the three-foot embankment in an attempt to retain her footing, gaining momentum as she lurched wildly down the slope, only stopping when she crashed into Matt and toppled both of them into the ditch.

"Are you all right?" Matt gasped.

She realized with a shock that he lay under her. She could feel the hardness of his chest, the muscle of his thighs, the heat of his hands beside her breasts. His face was so close to hers that his beard rasped her chin and his breath warmed her cheek. It smelled faintly of root beer and Juicy Fruit gum, a combination she found unexpectedly erotic.

"Yes," she breathed. "Are you?"

Golden eyes poured into hers. The blood in her veins suddenly seemed warmer and thicker and faster, pumping through her body in double time.

Her pulse pounded in her ears and she wasn't sure she could breathe. *Maybe I'll pass out,* she thought wildly. *Maybe I'd be better off if I did.*

Her gaze fell on his mouth. His lips were slightly parted and close—so very close. They looked full and firm and... delicious. Was he going to kiss her?

"Yes," he said thickly.

She thought he was reading her mind. It took her a moment to realize he was responding to her earlier question.

His fingers tightened almost imperceptibly on her ribs, and she glanced up again at his eyes. The desire she saw there was a mirror of her own. His gaze slid slowly to her lips. His mouth did the same.

The contact was everything she remembered and more—explosive, jarring, melting. She·parted her lips and closed her eyes, awash in ripples of sweet heat. His tongue demanded entrance. She granted it and moved against him, mindlessly seeking relief for the aching need building within her. His fingers slid upward and she moaned with pleasure. She was oblivious to everything but Matt's hard, firm body beneath her, his mouth moving on hers, his hands doing the very things she'd fantasized.

The sound of an approaching truck engine vaguely entered her consciousness. "Someone's coming," he whispered abruptly. "I'll help you up."

A pair of strong arms pushed her up and off. Disoriented, Ali opened her eyes as she landed in a sitting position. Matt stood above her, stretching down a hand. She reflexively reached up for it and let him haul her to her feet.

She stood just as a green pickup with the Cimarron Homebuilders logo on the door rounded the corner. Matt waved to the two employees inside, who stared at them with frankly curious expressions.

"That was a damn fool stunt you just pulled," he said in a tight voice.

Ali felt heat suffuse her face from her neck to the roots of her hair. She had to admit she'd been shamelessly willing, but why was he placing all the blame on her?

"It so happens *you* kissed *me*," she retorted.

Matt jammed his hands into his pockets and shifted his weight uneasily. "That's not what I'm talking about—although it wouldn't have happened if you'd followed directions. Why didn't you wait in the truck and let me get the door for you?"

Ali crossed her arms defensively. She was still trying to recover from the breathless way his kiss had affected her. She lifted her head, met his blazing eyes and decided she'd give as good as she got. If he could channel his passion into anger, she could, too.

"There's no need to give me special treatment just because I'm a woman," she replied. "I'm your business partner, and I'm perfectly capable of opening my own doors."

Matt scowled and swatted a leaf off the sleeve of his jacket. "Yeah, and of knocking me down in the process." He slapped at his other sleeve and shot her a frown. "For your information, I wasn't trying to open the door just to be polite. I parked on an incline and I was trying to keep you from breaking your neck when you got out of the truck."

Heat flooded Ali's cheeks. "Well, why didn't you just say so?" she said indignantly.

Matt shrugged and pulled his hands from his pockets. "I didn't know I needed to. I hadn't figured you for the type to get offended at a simple courteous gesture."

The comment made Ali bristle. How dare he twist things around so that it was all her fault! He made her sound like the rudest sort of ingrate. Ali huffily turned away, only to find the house with the round turret directly in her line of vision. The sight put a damper on her indignation.

She needed to stay on peaceable terms with Matt if she were going to work with him. She couldn't afford to indulge her temper, and she definitely couldn't afford to tell him what she really thought of him and his high-handed ways.

It takes a strong person to admit a mistake, she reminded herself. She brushed a stray wisp of hair from her face, drew a deep, steadying breath and unclenched her teeth. "I didn't mean to hit you with the door," she forced herself to say. *Even if it did serve you right.*

Her admission seemed to catch him off guard. An expression of confusion and wariness flitted across his face and he raked a hand through his hair. "Well, I didn't mean to get carried away. It won't happen again," he mumbled. He looked away, then glanced back at her. "You'd better brush off your jacket. The framing foreman's coming and you're covered with leaves."

Ali wiped at her sleeve as an enormous man with the reddest complexion she'd ever seen approached.

Matt managed to put a smile on his face. "Hi, Jim. Looks like you've been busy out here." He pumped the man's hand and turned to Ali. "Ali, this is Jim Bentmore, our framing foreman. Most folks call him Big Jim. Jim, this is Robert's sister. She's going to be handling the interior design of the first three houses."

Jim smiled broadly and doffed his baseball cap. "Well, well. Nice to meet you, ma'am."

"It's my pleasure," Ali replied, immediately liking the man's open, friendly face. She cast a quick glance at Matt, surprised that he had so graciously introduced her in her new role. She'd halfway expected him to downplay the part she was going to play in the development.

"I thought the world of your brother," Big Jim was saying, his brown eyes warm and sincere. He turned to Matt and nodded. "Good idea, getting a woman's touch. After all, the ladies always have the final say on pickin' out a new home. Smart thinkin', Matt!"

Matt looked anxious to change the topic. "Yeah, well . . ." he muttered. "Let's go take a look at how things are coming along."

The path was narrow and they trudged along in single file as they wended their way through the trees to the house. Ali followed behind Jim, glad to have another person along to act as a buffer.

She had just begun to relax her tensed muscles when she felt a warm brush against her back. She was certain it wasn't an overhanging branch; a tree would never cause that tingling sensation to shoot up her spine. It was the same telling thrill that raced through her every time Matt touched her.

Ali turned around sharply. Matt raised an eyebrow and held up two leaves he'd evidently just plucked off her coat. Ali scurried to catch up with Jim. There was something unnervingly intimate about Matt brushing off her clothes—especially when he was doing it so surreptitiously. He acted as if they had a secret to keep—as though they'd been lying in the leaves like lovers.

Which they had. Ali's pulse still throbbed with the force of her desire. She'd nearly lost her head, despite the fact it was broad daylight and they'd been in plain sight of the road. She'd been so overwhelmed she'd lost all track of time and space.

She was certain Matt had, too. That was probably why he'd gotten so angry at her—the attraction had been too intense, his reaction too heated and primal. He no doubt blamed her for his own irrational behavior.

Confound him anyway! And confound her for being so drawn to his infuriating, bossy, know-it-all self.

She was just going to have to keep a tight rein on her behavior. She might not be able to control her feelings, but she could definitely control her actions. And it was important that she behave in a reasonable, rational fashion around Matt. If he didn't take her seriously, she would have an uphill battle getting him to approve her designs for the houses.

Besides, why would she want to get romantically involved with an impossible, domineering, have-an-answer-for-everything male like Matt Jordan? She wanted to stand on her own two feet, to be in charge of her own life and her own decisions, to have her ideas respected. She didn't want someone telling her what to do or treating her like a scatterbrain.

Ali felt Matt take another slap at the back of her jacket and quickened her stride to catch up with Jim. The more distance she kept between herself and Matt Jordan, the better off she was going to be.

Matt took a sip of coffee and grimaced. "What the heck have you done to the coffee, Hattie?"

Hattie pushed a file across his desk and peered over the top of her glasses at him. "Don't you like it?" she asked mildly.

Matt wrinkled his nose. "It doesn't taste normal."

Hattie sorted through the stack of papers in his Out box. "Everyone else thinks it's delicious."

Matt took another cautious sip. "What did you do to it?" he repeated.

"Actually, nothing." Hattie picked up a manila envelope and flattened the fastener on it. "Ali made it."

Matt rolled his eyes and Hattie shot him a disapproving look. "I thought it was delightful," she said. "It's a flavored blend—Amaretto Mocha Cherry Cordial Creme."

"What kind of coffee is that for an office?" Matt demanded. "It tastes like it ought to have one of those little umbrellas floating in it."

"I think it's a pleasant change," Hattie replied.

"Who said the coffee needed to be changed?" Matt groused.

Hattie's expression told Matt she was clearly exasperated. "I'll make you a separate pot if you like."

The offer made Matt feel petty. "Don't bother," he muttered. "You've got more important things to do."

"Sometimes a little change is good for the soul, Matt." She leveled a knowing look at him and sauntered out of his office.

Matt expelled a heavy breath the moment the door closed behind her. If that were the case, his soul should be in prime condition, he thought glumly. Pushing back his chair, he stood and strode to the window, shoving a lock of hair away from his forehead.

Ali had only been here two weeks and her "little changes" were driving him crazy. A new surprise confronted him everywhere he turned, and he hated surprises. He'd had enough of those to last a lifetime when he was a child, and he placed a high value on order and consistency and reliability.

It wasn't that the changes were all bad ones, he thought begrudgingly, but they sure weren't necessary, either.

In the past two weeks Ali had rearranged everything from the stacks of paper by the copy machine to the pens and pencils in the supply closet. Robert's old office was completely unrecognizable with its new rugs and lamps and pictures, and the coffee break room now had a soda pop machine that Ali had convinced a local vending machine company to install. The reception area boasted a floral arrangement, the telephone played music whenever the hold button was pressed and the conference room sported a palm tree in the corner. She'd even managed to make the men's room smell like baby powder.

The most maddening aspect of it all was that the staff seemed to love it. In fact, her decorating zeal seemed to be contagious; work areas were being spruced up throughout the office building and grounds. Yesterday he'd even caught Jim Bentmore sweeping out the storage shed at the back of the equipment yard.

Matt frowned. He didn't like it—not one little bit. It was bad enough he had to act like a hermit, hiding out in his office to avoid her. His body had become a traitor; just seeing her set him on edge, interfered with his ability to concentrate and sent his thoughts down distinctly lustful paths. Not seeing her didn't eradicate the condition, but at least it kept it from escalating.

Well, he might have to temporarily put up with having her at the office, but he didn't have to put up with total upheaval. Each change she'd made had seemed so benign at the time that he'd let it go unchallenged, but they'd added up to the point where he felt like a stranger in his own place of business.

Matt's jaw settled into a determined line. The situation was completely out of control. It was time he had a talk with her, Matt thought firmly. She needed to know exactly who was in charge here.

He strode purposefully down the hall to Ali's office only to find the door open but the room empty. Matt looked around at the pastel pictures, the plush rug, the dried flower arrangement on the credenza and the other feminine touches, and shook his head. It was hard to even remember what this room had looked like before.

Where could she be?

"Anywhere, doing anything," Matt muttered. For all he knew, today's project might involve stenciling daffodils on the ceiling. He'd start with the conference room; maybe she was arranging lace throw pillows on the leather chairs.

Matt thrust open the door to the conference room and stopped dead in his tracks. Gathered around the table was the oddest assortment of people he'd ever seen.

Two identical elderly ladies in identical pink flowered dresses sat on opposite sides of the table. Matt looked at one, then the other, then back again, thinking they were some kind of mirror trick. They were both as plump as roasting hens and had brightly rouged cheeks that bobbed like apples above their mutiple chins.

A thin, sour-faced man with a waxed handlebar mustache sat next to one of them, and a bearded gentleman dressed like Abraham Lincoln sat beside the other. To his right was a young woman with spiky pink hair and a nose ring.

At one end of the table sat the mayor of Hillsboro, and at the other end, looking as if she were presiding over a meeting of Fortune Five Hundred executives, sat Ali.

"Oh, uh, excuse me." Matt started to back out of the room, anxious to beat a retreat and close the door on the lot of them.

"Matt, come in," Ali said. She fixed him with a smile of such blinding intensity that he froze like a frog in a flashlight beam.

Matt kept his hand on the doorknob as Ali turned to the motley group. "I'd like to introduce Matt Jordan, the president of our company. Matt, I'd like you to meet our showcase committee." She nodded her head toward one of the rosy-cheeked women. "This is Fay Hawthorne, and her sister, Gay. They own the local bed, bath and fabric store, Suds 'n Duds.

They're going to loan us bed and bath furnishings. They've also generously agreed to custom-make the draperies at cost."

"Oo-oh, it's a pleasure to meet you," one tittered in a high-pitched voice as she batted her eyes at him.

"I'm sure," the other simpered.

Matt shifted uncomfortably and tried not to stare. "Nice to meet you," he mumbled.

Ali stretched a hand toward the Lincolnesque character. "This is Charles Goodson. He owns Good Ole Time Antiques. He's going to loan us some of the furniture for the show homes. He's also offered to provide us with period costumes for the hostesses to wear."

"Uh, great," Matt said. *Hostesses? What the hell was she talking about?*

"This is Nathan Bradley of Bradley Furniture. He's going to loan us appliances and the rest of the furnishings."

Matt forced himself to smile in response to the man's curt nod.

"And this is Jamie Zumwaldt. She runs the Starving Artists Art Gallery and she's offered to provide artwork."

The pink-haired girl raised two fingers of a gloved hand. "Yo."

Matt swallowed hard. "Um . . . yo," he repeated.

"And I believe you know the mayor, Aaron Moxie."

"The Victorian Village will be a fine addition to our fair city," the mayor intoned, mopping his bald crown with a handkerchief. "Just the ticket to put Hillsboro on the map. Nice to see you again, Matt."

"Uh, good to see you, too, Mayor," Matt said.

"Why don't you pull up a chair and join us, Matt?" Ali asked.

"No!" The word came out fast and harsh. Matt ran his fingers through his hair and tried to modulate his voice. "I mean, I have another appointment and I'm running late." He curled his lips and hoped it would pass for a smile. "Nice to meet all of you. Have a good meeting."

Matt ducked out the door before anyone could protest and rapidly strode down the hall to his office. He grabbed his jacket from a hanger on the back of the door and stopped by Hattie's desk.

"I'm going to the job site," he told her.

Hattie looked up in surprise. "Is something the matter there?"

"No," Matt said. "Why?"

"Because you're a creature of habit, and you never visit the job site at his time of day."

The comment sent a ripple of surprise through Matt. His life was orderly, yes, but was he really so predictable? His eyes narrowed as his mouth tightened into a frown. He didn't like that "creature of habit" label. It made him sound staid and stuffy and stuck in a rut—like an old man.

Hattie was giving him a searching look. "Will you be gone long?"

Matt jerked his head toward the conference room. "Depends. How long do you think Ali's little tea party in there is likely to last?"

"So that's it." Hattie gave an amused grin. "They'll probably break up in less than half an hour. The Hawthorne sisters never miss a meal and it's getting close to lunchtime."

Matt drummed his fingers thoughtfully on Hattie's desk. He needed to approach Ali carefully. He'd learned the hard way that simply demanding she do things his way didn't work. Maybe he should try to catch this fly with honey. "Do you happen to know if Ali has any plans for lunch?"

"I know she put a carton of yogurt and half a sandwich in the refrigerator this morning," Hattie replied.

Matt straightened and buttoned his jacket. "When her meeting breaks up, would you please ask her to join me at the Mexicali Café?"

"For lunch?"

Matt scowled. "Why else would I invite her there?"

Hattie raised her eyebrows till they were visible over the rim of her glasses. "I don't know. Judging from the look on your face, it might be to bite her head off. Besides, it's not like you to make a lunch date on the spur of the moment."

Matt shoved his hands into his pockets and deepened his frown. "Just because I like to plan things out doesn't mean I'm not capable of an occasional spontaneous gesture."

Hattie gave him a complacent smile. "I'm glad to hear it. I'm sure Ali will be, too."

Matt eyed her warily. "Just give her the message, will you please?" he said tersely, marching toward the exit.

Boy, he missed Robert! He was surrounded by people who seemed to prefer reckless change and pandemonium to an orderly existence. Robert had liked a well-ordered life nearly as much as he did, and Matt missed having an ally.

How had a rational, logical person like Robert ended up with such an unruly creature for a sister? Matt wished he knew how Robert had dealt with her. Probably the same way he'd handled architectural problems, Matt thought—with creative solutions. If one way didn't work, he'd try something different.

Matt unlocked his car door and slid behind the steering wheel. Well, that was exactly what he intended to do—approach Ali from a new angle. He'd buy her lunch, pay her a few compliments, and try to convince her that all of her future actions on behalf of Cimarron Homebuilders needed to be cleared through him.

How hard could that be?

Ali squinted as she followed the hostess to Matt's table, her eyes trying to adjust to the dim restaurant lighting after the brilliance of the noonday sunshine.

"Hello," Matt said, jumping up and circling the table to pull out her chair. "I'm glad you could join me."

Her vision cleared enough to see his eyes scan her legs as she seated herself. Her heart picked up speed as a surge of attraction rushed through her, the same attraction she felt every time she saw him. Aware that he was still eyeing her legs, she tugged at her skirt and tried to hide her pounding pulse with a calm facade. "Thanks for inviting me," she said.

She busied herself unfolding her napkin, trying to figure out what Matt was up to. Inviting her to lunch in a dimly lit restaurant in the middle of a workday was certainly out of character. Especially since she was certain he'd been deliberately avoiding her. He'd taken to keeping the door to his office closed and he was always in a hurry when she passed him in the hall.

All of which was fine with her, she reminded herself. She didn't need the distraction of a physical attraction in the workplace—an attraction that even now was making her palms grow damp.

"What's the occasion?" Ali asked.

Matt rested his forearms on the table. "Does there have to be a special occasion for me to invite you to lunch?" His voice had a defensive edge.

"I suppose not. But it's not in keeping with your regular schedule."

Matt knit his brows together. It was the second time today the topic of his regular schedule had come up. Was he really such a creature of habit? "What do you know about my regular schedule?" he asked.

Ali answered by glancing at her watch. "It's now twelve-thirty—precisely the time of day you head out the door for the Cattlemen's Café, where you order the blue plate special. Since this is Friday, that would be fried catfish with hushpuppies."

Matt stared at her, aghast. "And just how would you happen to know a thing like that?" he demanded.

"I had lunch there earlier in the week and got into a conversation with the waitress. She asked where I worked and I told her." Ali grinned at him. "She told me you were her best customer."

Matt scowled. He didn't like the idea that his habits were suddenly a topic of conversation everywhere he turned.

"I was with Susan," Ali continued. "She and Hank are back from their honeymoon. They had a wonderful time."

"Glad to hear it." Was he really such a fuddy-duddy? Ali made him sound as stuffy as a taxidermist's parlor. Was that how she saw him?

Ali picked up a tortilla chip and dipped it into a bowl of salsa. "Susan looks terrific. Marriage really seems to agree with her." Ali took a bite and cast an inquisitive glance at Matt. "How long were you married, Matt?"

The question caught him off guard, and he answered it without thinking. "Less than a year. That was ten years ago."

Ali leaned forward, her gray eyes sparkling with curiosity. "Really? What happened?"

Matt shrugged in a display of nonchalance, still smarting from her uncannily accurate account of his noontime schedule. It wouldn't hurt to let her know that parts of his life weren't so staid and predictable. "We didn't want the same things out of life—so she left me for someone who could keep her in the style to which she wanted to become accustomed."

"Oh, I'm sorry," Ali murmured. "I didn't mean to bring up a painful subject."

Matt was surprised at the depth of concern reflected in her soft eyes. "It's not painful. Not anymore. It's nothing but a mistake in my past I don't intend to repeat." He eyed her speculatively. "How about you? Why aren't you married?"

Ali toyed with the corner of her cloth napkin. "I came close a couple of years ago—until he started trying to make me over. He didn't like my car or my clothes or the way I wear my hair."

"I like your clothes and your hair just fine." The words surprised Matt as much as Ali. He watched a rush of color flood her face, and felt a corresponding rush of pleasure at having caused it. "I don't know about your car."

Ali plucked a piece of lint off the tablecloth, a smile playing on her lips. "Trust me, you wouldn't like it, either. But those things weren't really the issue. They just made me realize that he wasn't looking for an equal partner. I saw that sort of lopsided relationship up close in my parents' marriage, and it's not for me."

Matt looked at her in surprise. "But Robert always talked about your dad like he hung the moon."

Ali nodded. "Robert thought he did. He patterned himself after him." Ali propped her elbows on the table and rested her chin on her hands. "Don't get me wrong—Dad was a great guy. But he was nearly twenty years older than Mom and he kept her in the dark about a lot of things. Mom didn't even know how to write a check. He doled out an allowance to her. When he died, there were a lot of debts Mom didn't know about, and we ended up losing our home."

"Robert told me about that. It must have been rough."

Ali nodded. "Dad died when I was nine and Robert was fourteen. Thank goodness Mom was a fast learner. She was able to pick up the pieces and build a new life, but it wasn't easy. Mom started baby-sitting children in our apartment and eventually opened her own day-care center. But we were on food stamps for a while there. I determined then and there that I would never again take charity, and I swore I'd never be dependent on anyone like my mother was."

Ali toyed with her flatware, carefully lining up the knife and spoon with the edge of her plate. Matt watched thoughtfully, realigning his perception of her.

She'd been serious when she'd told him earlier that she didn't want to take half the proceeds from the development without doing half the work, he realized. She hated the idea of taking something she hadn't earned or being dependent on someone else. Hell, he thought, running a hand through his hair, even the changes she'd made at the office were probably the result of her need to feel like a contributing partner.

The revelation put all of her efforts into a different perspective. It made her seem likeable, understandable, rational.

And more appealing than ever. His eyes rested on her with new admiration.

Ali looked up to meet his gaze. "What about you? What was your childhood like?"

She'd been so empathetic about his marriage that for once he found he didn't mind talking about it. "We didn't have any serious money problems, but it wasn't easy," he confessed. "My father had a sales job that kept him on the road a lot and Mom was a teacher. When he was home, he was more interested in playing golf with his buddies than spending time with Mom and me. My childhood memories are mainly of half kept or broken promises—the model car we were going to build together that was still in its box when I went to college. The time when I was six and waited for him to come home and take me to the circus, and he forgot. I waited by the door from noon until bedtime.''

"Oh, Matt." Ali's eyes again had that soft, caring light, and a comforting warmth spread through his chest. "Did you have any brothers or sisters?"

"No. I always wished I did. I wanted someone to help me take care of Mom, to cheer her up." Matt exhaled forcefully. "Dad disappointed her even more often than me. He left her for a younger woman when I was sixteen. We got word a year later he'd died of a heart attack." Matt looked down at his hand on the table and curled his fingers into a fist. "It was the first word we'd had of him since he'd left."

"What happened to your mother?" Ali asked.

Matt leaned forward and looked up. "She remarried three years later. Fred is terrific."

"Where are they now?" Ali asked.

"In Florida. They retired and moved there a couple of years ago."

Ali regarded him pensively. "So you're the exact opposite of your father."

"I sure hope so. That's always been my intention." Matt met Ali's eyes and another thread of connectedness wove between them, strengthening the lariat of attraction that spun around them. The warmth in his chest spread lower, and he impulsively laid his hand over hers on the tabletop. "And you're the opposite of your mother. What a pair we make."

Did Matt really think of them as a pair? The thought made Ali's stomach tighten. She could tell it had been hard for him to talk about his childhood. Tenderness welled up within her, tenderness heightened by the thought of him as a little boy, dressed up and excited about the circus, waiting by the door for a daddy who never showed.

His need to stay in control, his affinity for order, his desire to plan things out and follow the plan—they all sprang from the broken heart of that jilted little boy.

The revelation made Ali's own heart ache. She wanted to take him in her arms, hold him close and fulfill all the promises other people had made and broken.

The thought shocked her. What was she thinking? He wasn't a little boy she could harmlessly cuddle. He was a full grown man—a man who was holding her hand in a dimly lit restaurant in the middle of the day, a virile, attractive man who made her stomach flutter and her pulse race and her head swim.

A waitress approached the table and Ali felt a sense of both loss and relief when Matt withdrew his hand. Loss because touching him thrilled and excited her; relief because those very feelings made it hard to think.

"Do you need some time to look at the menu?" Matt asked.

Ali shook her head. "I'll take the enchilada plate and an iced tea. And if you have any hotter salsa, I'd like some, please."

"I'll have the same thing," Matt said.

"Two enchilada platters and a bowl of Diablo salsa coming up," the waitress replied as she took the menus from them.

Matt took a sip of water and glanced at Ali. This outing was not going at all as he'd planned. He'd intended to address the changes she was making at the company, and instead the conversation had taken a distinctly personal turn. He'd just told her things about his childhood he hadn't even told her brother. The exchange somehow put their relationship on a different footing.

Maybe he should just drop the whole topic of the changes she'd made at the office. Now that he thought about it, they really weren't such a big deal. Besides, he didn't like the fact that she evidently shared Hattie's perception of him as rigid and inflexible.

"What do you think about the changes I've made at the office?" Ali asked.

The woman had radar for trouble. Matt shifted uneasily in his chair.

"There, uh, have been a few," he said noncommittally.

Ali nodded. "I probably should have consulted you, but you seemed so busy I hated to disturb you. I saw a few little things that I thought would make the office environment a little more pleasant, so I just went ahead and did them. You don't mind, do you?"

Matt had been studying her face distractedly as she talked, taking in her delicate cheekbones, her pert nose, her large, beautiful, sincere gray eyes. He lowered his gaze to her mouth, to the full, ripe voluptuousness of her lips.

He shook his head. "No," he murmured. "I don't mind."

And at the moment he truly didn't. Not at all.

The thought caused him a surge of alarm, and he was glad when the waitress appeared with their order. He dug his fork into the guacamole salad and decided to broach a new topic.

"How are your interior designs coming?" Matt asked, lifting a bite to his mouth.

"Great," Ali said, spooning a huge helping of hot sauce onto a soft tortilla. "I'm nearly done with the boards for the first house."

"Boards?"

"Large cardboard sheets showing the design elements for each room—paint chips, wallpaper samples, photos of lighting, fixtures, et cetera. I want to get them finished before I show them to you so you can see the full picture. I'm waiting on a set of wallpaper samples, but they should be in next week. You'll be happy to know that the estimates are coming in under budget."

"Glad to hear it," Matt said.

"Speaking of interiors—I'm ready to start painting my living room this weekend. Do you still want to volunteer?"

Matt swallowed a bite of Spanish rice as an alarm bell went off in his mind. *Don't get personally involved*, it warned. *You can easily assign one of your workmen.*

But really, what could it hurt if he helped her?

"Sure. I'll come by around nine." He scooped up some salsa on a tortilla chip and popped it into his mouth.

Jumpin' jalapeños! What had he just bitten into? His tongue burned like a six-alarm fire. His eyes watered and he groped blindly on the table for a glass.

"Are you all right, Matt?"

He struggled to form a word, his hands desperately roving the tabletop for something to extinguish the inferno in his mouth. "Wa— Wa— Water," he gasped.

"Are you choking?"

His vision was so blurred that he could barely make out her face as she leaned across the table. Sweat beading on his brow, he shook his head and continued to search the table for a glass. His fingers closed around one and he jerked it to his mouth.

Empty. Oh, jeez, he was in agony. He grabbed another glass. Empty, too. How could both their water *and* iced tea glasses be dry as bones? Where was the waitress?

"Pl-please get wa-water," he croaked.

Ali was out of her chair. *Oh, thank heavens. She's gone to get me a drink,* he thought.

He was mentally calling her an angel of mercy when something slammed him hard in the gut, knocking the breath out of him.

"Ugh!" he grunted, doubling over and clutching his stomach.

"Are you better?" Ali's voice came from behind his chair. He realized her arms were wrapped around him, one of them knotted into a fist and pressed against his belly.

Hell's bells! She's doing the Heimlich maneuver on me! Oh, criminy, she'll do it again if I don't stop her.

Matt grabbed both her wrists. "Not choking," he croaked.

The waitress appeared, a water pitcher in her hands. She cracked her gum and stared down at them. "Can I help you?"

"Wa-water," Matt managed.

She took a maddeningly long time to pour it, then stood with a hand on her hip and watched him drain the glass in a single gulp. She leaned over to refill it, still smacking her gum. "The raw cayenne and jalapeño peppers in that Diablo salsa give it quite a punch. Too hot for a lot of people." Matt downed the glass, and she sloshed water into it again. "Never saw anyone have a reaction like you, though."

Ali crouched beside him, her eyes dark with worry. "Are you okay?"

Matt drew a deep breath and wiped his brow. His mouth still felt like the inside of an incinerator, but he no longer thought he was in danger of exploding.

Except perhaps at Ali. He must have lost his mind—discussing his childhood, okaying the changes she'd made at the office, feeling so warm and comfortable and...and...*intimate* with her. For a while there, he'd forgotten she was the very essence of trouble.

Well, it hadn't taken long before she'd reminded him. Matt turned and glared at her. "What the hell did you do that for?"

Ali backed away and put the table between them, lowering herself to her seat. "I thought you were choking."

"I told you I wasn't," he snapped. "Why didn't you just get me some water like I asked?"

Ali turned both palms up. "Sometimes people who're choking don't realize how serious the situation is until it's too late. You got so red in the face I was worried." She gave him an apologetic smile. "I figured it was better to be safe than sorry."

How could he argue with that? The fact that he couldn't find fault with her logic irritated him all the more.

"Well, why did you order that stuff? And how in blazes did you manage to eat any of it? That junk ought to be registered with a nuclear regulatory agency."

Ali laughed. "I love spicy food. I eat it all the time, so I guess I've built up a tolerance to it." She leaned forward and touched his hand. "I'm really sorry, Matt. Did I hurt you?"

Matt gingerly felt his stomach. She might have bruised a rib, but he'd be darned if he'd let her know it.'

"Nah. I'm pretty tough." *At least, I used to be before you hit town.*

Matt took another gulp of water, eyeing her warily over the rim. The girl was like a force of nature; he never knew when or where she was going to strike next. He ought to run for cover every time she got within twenty paces.

The odd part was, in spite of everything, he didn't want to put distance between them. He wanted to get closer—a lot closer. He glanced down at her small hand on top of his and a

110 THE WEDDING KISS

surge of desire flashed through him. *I never knew I had such a self-destructive bent,* he thought derisively.

Matt sighed deeply. How the heck was he going to survive until the development was completed?

Chapter Eight

Ali stood in the middle of her living room, her hands on her hips, and gazed around at her handiwork. All of the furniture had been dragged into the center of the room and covered with sheets. Heavy plastic covered the floor, tape edged the windows, the walls were bare of pictures and Spackle surface compound filled every nail hole.

"Looks like we're ready for the painting party to begin," Ali told Flipper. The little dog wagged his tail in response from his perch on the back of the sheet-draped sofa.

Ali glanced at her watch; she still had ten minutes before Matt was due to arrive—enough time to check her hair and maybe even put on some lipstick. Not that she really cared about her appearance, she told herself as she headed for her bedroom, Flipper at her heels. She just wanted to look presentable, that was all.

Sure, Ali, sure, another part of her mind mocked. She'd already changed clothes three times this morning before deciding she was *not* going to make any concessions to this insane attraction she felt for Matt Jordan. After all, she was dressing to paint her living room wall, not stroll down a fashion show runway.

Besides, it was pointless. A relationship with Matt would do nothing but complicate her life.

Ali rummaged through the drawer of her vanity table for her lipstick and sighed. There was no denying that she was attracted to the man—and he'd never seemed more attractive than when he'd opened up to her yesterday. For a few minutes there, he'd been approachable and warm and emotionally available. Knowing why he had such a need to maintain order and control made him a lot less intimidating, a lot more appealing.

Not that he needed to be any more appealing—especially when he wore that sexy combination of casual and business attire like he had yesterday. Who would have thought that a starched Oxford shirt, faded jeans and a tweed jacket could look so devastating? And when she'd put her arms around him to perform the Heimlich maneuver, his hard, taut stomach had had plenty of appeal, too.

Thinking of the Heimlich maneuver episode made her scrunch her face into a scowl. *Matt must think I'm a real nut case,* she thought ruefully.

"Well, he *did* look like he was choking," Ali muttered defensively. "Anyone could have made the same mistake."

But it hadn't been anyone, it had been her. She winced as she tallied up the number of offenses she'd committed against him.

"He probably regards me as the human equivalent of a black cat," she told Flipper remorsefully.

Flipper lifted his head from her bed and whined.

Ali frowned at her reflection. She'd long ago accepted that chaos was just a part of her life. She seemed to attract it, like other people attracted good luck or stray animals. Her private theory was that it all had to do with personal electromagnetic fields.

But Matt wasn't the sort of man who wanted random forces of the universe tampering with his carefully laid-out plans. And after hearing how his father's lack of responsibility had tainted his childhood, she couldn't blame him. He'd been dis-

appointed so many times when he was young that it was easy
to understand why he hated surprises now.

Ali replaced the lid on her lipstick and firmly closed the
drawer. Why was she so concerned about what Matt thought
about her, anyway? Regardless of how understandable his
reasons were, the fact remained that Matt was rigid and domineering, and she'd sworn to never get involved with that type
of man.

She did have to work with him, however, and she would be
at a definite disadvantage if he believed she was an airhead.
She needed to keep in mind that he had veto power over everything she proposed.

The thought sent a shiver of apprehension through her. He'd
said he wouldn't approve anything he considered farfetched or
out of line, and there was no telling how conservative he was
going to be. After all, his idea of interior decor was white walls
and tan carpet. If he didn't have confidence in her, he wasn't
likely to have any confidence in her work.

Well, there was nothing she could do about the gaffes she'd
already committed, but from now on, she'd try extra hard to
make her encounters with Matt as trouble-free as possible.
She'd try her darnedest to make sure no accidents occurred
today.

The doorbell interrupted her thoughts. Flipper barked
sharply and hurled himself off the bed in a backward somersault, then trotted after her down the hall.

Matt's gaze traveled over her as she opened the door. He'd
never thought of a sweatsuit as a particularly alluring set of
clothing, but Ali sure made it look that way. The blue fabric
molded to her slim hips and full breasts in a way that made his
pulse pound. Her soft, intoxicating scent wafted toward him,
and he wondered where she applied her perfume. He'd sure
like to find out.

Stop it, Jordan, he reprimanded himself. He was here to
help her paint and nothing else.

He raised two fingers to his forehead in a mock salute and
gave her a grin. "Handy Dandy Painters at your service,
ma'am."

She smiled, her gray eyes shining like sunshine on a lake. "It's really nice of you to help with this, Matt."

"No problem." He gestured toward his truck. "I brought some equipment. Why don't I bring it in?"

She stepped back from the door. "Great. While you're doing that, I'll give Flipper some toys to keep him out of our way."

Matt gathered a collection of brushes, rollers and plastic sheeting from the bed of his truck and lugged them to the living room. He set them down, straightened and looked around in surprise.

Jiminy—Ali seemed to have thought of everything! He'd fully expected to have to prepare the room from scratch and make two or three runs to the store for things they lacked. Instead, it looked like the room had been outfitted by a professional paint contractor.

Matt took it all in, then crossed the room to study the assorted equipment Ali had neatly laid out in the corner. He was staring at an odd piece of equipment he didn't recognize when Ali came into the room.

"Ready to get started?" Ali asked.

"Sure," Matt replied. "But what's this?" He pointed to a long plastic strip attached to a handle.

"That?" Ali hesitated a heartbeat. "It's a paint slinger."

"A what?"

"A paint slinger." She turned innocent eyes on him. "If you get tired of painting with a roller, you can use it to hurl globs of paint at the wall."

All Matt could do was stare.

Ali laughed. "Just kidding. Actually, I use it to keep paint off the ceiling." She picked it up by the handle, raised it over her head and pressed it against the ceiling where it met the wall. "See? It acts as a shield."

"Oh," Matt said, a little taken aback. He hadn't expected Ali to be so well organized or farsighted. "That's clever."

Ali shrugged. "It's usually used to smooth wallpaper, but I've found it has lots of uses."

Matt glanced at her with renewed respect as he knelt to open a can of paint. There was more to Ali than he'd initially figured.

A lot more, Matt thought by the time noon arrived. Ali had supervised their activities with the precision of a field sergeant, but with none of the accompanying bossiness. Her directions had been so tactfully issued that if he hadn't been consciously evaluating her every move, he would have thought he was running the show.

"Ready for lunch?" Ali asked from her perch on the step-ladder.

"That depends." Matt stood under her, holding the ceiling gizmo, enjoying the view of her feminine assets from this unusual angle. He gave her a teasing grin. "Are you planning to perform the Heimlich maneuver on me?"

Ali turned slightly on the ladder, her lips curved in amusement. "I don't know yet. Are you going to act like you're choking?"

"Only if you're serving hot sauce."

Ali laughed as she climbed down, and Matt placed his hands on her waist to help her with the last two steps. She gave a sharp intake of breath as his fingers touched her and faltered slightly as she hit the ground, pressing the length of her body against him.

Attraction shot through him like an arrow. He didn't take the socially correct step backward that would have put them a polite distance from each other—but then, neither did she.

Matt's heart sledgehammered against his chest. Her breath was soft and warm on his face, her eyes dark and heavy-lidded, her lips a sweet, irresistible temptation. He was about to give in to it when something hit him upside the head.

Matt jerked back, his hand on the injury. "What the devil was that?"

"Flipper."

Matt stared down at the dog, who was chasing a small blue ball across the plastic-covered carpet. The little beast grabbed it in his tiny teeth, turned his head and hurled it. This time,

Matt caught it in midair. Flipper barked and performed a back flip.

Ali laughed. "He wants to play catch. He throws and you catch."

"With normal dogs, it's the other way around."

"There's nothing normal about Flipper," she said proudly.

Matt rolled his eyes. "You can say that again."

Ali smiled and tucked a strand of hair behind her ear. "He must really like you, Matt. He doesn't play with just anyone."

"Lucky me," Matt said dryly, rubbing the spot the ball had struck.

Ali stepped toward the kitchen. "If you'll put the lid on the paint, I'll get lunch ready."

Matt eyed the dog as he tended to the task. The mongrel's timing was either terrible or brilliant—he wasn't sure which.

He found Ali in the kitchen a moment later pulling a ceramic bowl from the refrigerator. He took it from her and lifted the lid. "Mmm ... potato salad. One of my favorites," he said appreciatively.

Ali gave him a warm smile as she handed him platters of cold fried chicken and three-bean salad. "I figured the least I could do was provide you with a homecooked meal in exchange for your help." She closed the refrigerator and pulled some serving spoons from a drawer. "Why don't we eat outside? It's the first warm day of spring and it's a shame to spend all of it inside."

"Sounds good to me," Matt agreed. "What can I do to help?"

"There's an old quilt in the trunk at the foot of my bed. Would you mind getting it and finding us a sunny spot in the backyard?"

Matt set off down the hall, stopping short the moment he entered her bedroom. It was dominated by a large, four-poster bed covered with a beautiful pastel quilt. Plump pillows of all sizes nestled invitingly against the headboard, and an eyelet dust ruffle peeked out the bottom like a petticoat. Beside the bed, a lace-draped table held a romance novel, an alarm clock and a pair of graceful crystal candlesticks.

The vision of Ali stretched out on the bed, her face bathed in candlelight, her hair flowing on one of the pillows, hit him like a physical blow, momentarily knocking the wind out of him. What would she look like dressed in something as sheer as the lace curtains that hung at the windows—or less?

His body responded to the thought. Muttering an oath, he strode to the trunk, yanked out a quilt and slammed down the lid.

She was getting to him. He'd been attracted to her from that first day in the bridal shop, and he'd thought he could subjugate his attraction. He'd tried a brotherly approach, but that had been impossible. He'd tried avoiding her, but that had proved impractical. And now, the more time he spent with her, the more time he *wanted* to spend with her.

Clutching the quilt, he turned and fled her bedroom as if the hounds of hell were nipping at his heels.

Ali dawdled in the kitchen, gathering up napkins, paper plates and flatware. Through the window, she could see Matt spreading the blanket on a sunny patch of ground in the center of the backyard.

Stop stalling, she reprimanded herself. *You've got to go out there and face him sooner or later.*

The encounter by the stepladder had shaken her to the core. The flash of desire had been so unexpected and strong that she'd felt defenseless against it. If Flipper hadn't interrupted, she was certain she would have abandoned all her good intentions.

Being alone with Matt was like playing with fire; she'd have to be careful if she didn't want to get burned. She carried the stack of supplies outside, feeling nervous and edgy and in no mood for a picnic.

As the food disappeared and the sunshine warmed Ali's back, however, she felt the tension fade from her shoulders. The conversation rambled over a wide range of topics and an easy, companionable rapport grew between them.

"This is great," Matt said as he spooned another helping of
beans onto his plate, then reached for his third piece of
chicken. "I didn't know you could cook. From the way Robert talked, I thought you were a disaster in the kitchen." His
hand suddenly froze on a drumstick. "Are you sure we're not
going to get ptomaine or something?"

Ali stuck out her tongue and gave him a playful swat on the
arm. "For your information, Robert's stories about my
cooking were all a little dated. I've improved quite a bit since
the tenth grade—and I'm practically an expert on preventing
food poisoning."

Matt's eyes gleamed playfully. "Oh, yeah? How many people did you have to kill to earn that status?"

"Since you're so worried about it, I guess you won't want
any of my chocolate chip cookies," Ali retorted.

Matt gave her a grin. "Did I mention I like to live on the
edge?"

Ali laughed and passed him a cookie. He took a bite and
stretched out on the blanket, his muscles bulging through the
cotton of his striped rugby shirt as he propped himself on an
elbow. He reminded Ali of a lion basking in the sun.

She took a sip of iced tea, trying to ignore the effect his pose
was having on her pulse rate, and searched her mind for a distracting topic. "You seem to know about all the flubs and foi-
bles of my youth. What about yours?"

"None of my mistakes were very funny."

She leaned back on her arms and stretched her legs out in
front of her. "Tell me anyway."

Matt rolled over and lay on his back, gazing up at the sky.
"The worst was my third grade science project. My father
promised to help me build a model of the solar system. I
bragged to my friends about how cool it was going to be, how
it was going to have motorized planets that revolved around
the sun."

Matt fell silent as he studied a large puffy cloud moving
slowly through the blue sky. "But of course, Dad never found
the time to do it. At the last minute, Mom tried to help me
fashion something out of Styrofoam sheets and wire, but it was

nothing like the razzmatazz invention I'd described to my buddies. I ditched it on the way to school and told everyone my project had short-circuited and caught on fire."

"Oh, Matt," Ali sympathized.

"No one believed me," Matt continued. "My teacher called my mother, and Mom's feelings were hurt. The whole situation was a mess. But I learned some valuable lessons from the experience. Not to lie. Not to brag. Not to rely on anyone else to do something that's your responsibility. I also learned the value of planning and time management."

"It's good you got something positive out of it," Ali said softly.

Matt placed his hands under his head. "It wasn't all positive. It wasn't easy learning I wasn't a very important part of my father's life, that I couldn't trust him, that someone I loved and looked up to could let me down like that."

Before she stopped to think what she was doing, Ali reached out a hand to Matt. Her heart was filled with a mixture of emotions that she'd never simultaneously experienced before—empathy and concern and admiration and something more, something stronger, something she didn't dare try to name.

Her hand landed on his chest. Matt started at the contact, then turned his face toward her, placing his own hand over hers. She could feel his heartbeat accelerate under her palm, and her own picked up speed to match it.

"I've never told that story to anyone," he said, rolling onto his side to look at her, his hand still holding hers against his chest.

The confession sent an odd thrill through Ali, touching a tender part of her heart, a part that shifted and expanded to make more room for him. The idea that he would confide something so revealing to her—and only her—made her feel privileged and trusted and humble and...

Scared. In a way that she couldn't quite define, it changed things.

Ali pulled her hand away and sat up suddenly, feigning an interest in Flipper's antics at the far side of the yard. Shaken and shaky, she was dangerously close to losing all sense of perspective and decorum.

She began gathering up the leftovers. "I'd better take these inside before you have real reason to worry about food poisoning."

"I'll help," Matt offered. He sat up and began stacking soggy paper plates and napkins.

"No!" In her eagerness to have some time alone to compose her emotions, the word came out harsher than she'd intended. She forced a note of lightness into her voice. "It'll just take me a moment to put these things away. Why don't you make a small dog happy and play catch with him like he wants?"

"Okay," Matt said, hoisting himself to his feet. "But if you're not done in five minutes, I'm coming in to help you."

Ali watched him carry the paper plates across the lawn and deposit them in the garbage can. The small, thoughtful gesture made her chest constrict.

She watched him toss the ball across the lawn, his shoulder muscles rippling. Flipper barked, Matt laughed, and Ali's heart pounded wildly. She wasn't sure what moved her more— the fact he was here helping her paint, the way he'd opened up and shared himself with her, or the smooth, masculine grace of his movements.

For heaven's sake, get a grip on yourself.

But the only things she seemed able to grip at the moment were the beans and the potato salad. Hugging the bowls to her chest, she lowered her head and beat a retreat indoors.

"Ta dah!" Ali took a final, flourishing swipe at the wall with a paint roller, then turned and smiled down from the ladder at Matt. "All done. How does it look?"

Matt looked around the room and rubbed his chin. The soft, rosy shade of terracotta Ali had selected didn't look bad. In fact, he thought with surprise, it looked downright nice.

"It looks a lot better than I thought it was going to look when we first started," he remarked.

"Don't go overboard with the compliments—it might go to my head," Ali said with a wry grin.

Matt shifted his stance and jabbed his hands into his pockets. "That didn't come out quite right. What I meant to say is, when we started painting, I thought it was going to look too girlish. But it doesn't. It looks great."

And so do you, Matt thought as she beamed down at him, her face paint-dabbled and wreathed in a mass of unruly curls. He'd never realized a woman could look so adorable when she was so disheveled. He'd always gone for the perfectly groomed, every-hair-in-place type, but the idea of a woman who wasn't afraid to get messed up had a sudden, new appeal.

"Thanks, Matt," Ali replied with an impish grin. "Although I'd like to point out that a girlish decor wouldn't be entirely inappropriate. In case you hadn't noticed, it just so happens I *am* a girl."

Matt's gaze scanned her form. "Oh, I noticed," he murmured. "I definitely noticed."

Her eyes widened and she opened her mouth as if to say something, then closed it abruptly and began making her way down the ladder. Her slender hips swayed as she descended, and her sweatshirt rode up above her waist, revealing a tempting flash of skin. Matt reached up to help her down, deliberately placing his hand on her bare midriff. Her skin was warm and soft and the texture of silk, and touching it sent a jolt of desire vibrating through him.

The look in his eyes made Ali's pulse quicken as she turned toward him. She self-consciously took a step back and brushed a stray curl from her eyes, unknowingly adding a new smudge of paint to her forehead.

She drew a deep breath, trying to quell her body's response to his fingers on her naked skin. *Don't let this attraction thing sidetrack you,* she warned herself. He'd just given her an opening to talk about her decorating philosophy, and she needed to take advantage of it. If she could convince him that they were on the same wavelength, it might make a difference in whether or not he approved her designs.

Ali took another step back and gave him an uncertain smile. "Actually, I understand what you mean about a living room being too feminine," she said, bending to place the paint roller in a tray of solvent. "I think a lot of women take the concept of adding a woman's touch too far. Men don't feel at home in rooms that are too frilly, just like women don't feel comfortable in rooms that are overly masculine."

Matt began cleaning off the other painting tools. "So what's the solution—keep everything gender neutral?"

Ali shook her head. "The most inviting rooms have elements of both sexes. I think the secret is to keep things balanced—to let masculine and feminine objects play off each other."

Matt's eyes darkened as he regarded her. "You make it sound very... sensual." His voice was low and husky.

Ali's pulse tripped like a snare drum. Tension arced between them, and she crossed her arms defensively across her chest, determined not to get off track. "Well, good interior design *is* sensual. It's made up of textures and colors and shapes—even smells and sounds. All those things can influence the quality of your life. For example, did you know that people are more apt to have an argument in a yellow room? Or that people have better appetites in red dining rooms?"

A playful glint lit his eyes. "And what is this particular color supposed to do to you?"

She could tell what it was doing to him. Ali took a protective step back and decided to sidestep the whole issue. "At the moment, it's making me thirsty. Would you like a soft drink?"

Matt laughed and glanced at his watch. "I would, but I'm afraid I'll have to drink mine on the road. I promised to stop by the job site and talk to the roofing contractor before he knocked off for the day." He gave Ali a curious look. "Where are you planning to stay tonight?"

A blush scalded Ali's face. *Surely he wasn't asking.... Was he?* She turned away, vigorously wiping a brush with a rag, and feigned nonchalance. "Right here. Why?"

"What about the paint fumes?"

Ali exhaled slowly, thankful she had played it cool. "I'll leave the windows open in here and close the door to my bedroom. It's far enough away that it shouldn't be a problem."

Matt frowned. "That's not a good idea, Ali. You can't turn on the burglar alarm with the windows open."

A wave of irritation surged through Ali. He sounded just like Robert—doubting her judgment, treating her as if she had no common sense, disapproving of her decisions, telling her what to do. Just when she'd nearly convinced herself she'd misjudged Matt, he reverted to form.

But that wasn't the only reason she was irritated. It was one thing for her to throw up a defense against the sexual tension that had sizzled between them all day, and quite another for him to ignore it altogether. There was something between them, and she'd thought . . .

Never mind what she'd thought. She lifted her chin slightly and fixed him with a cool stare. "I wasn't aware a crime wave was under way, but if there is, that's all the more reason I need to stay right here. I certainly don't want to leave the house unoccupied with the windows wide open."

Matt raked a hand through his hair, regarding her with a baffled expression. "We could swap houses for the night," he suggested. "You can stay at my place where it's nice and safe and the alarm system works, and I'll sleep here."

Ali glared at him stubbornly. "Matt, I'm not leaving this house tonight. Don't treat me like a child. Hillsboro, Oklahoma, is not exactly a hotbed of criminal activity. I'll be just fine."

Matt met her heated gaze unblinkingly. They stared at each other for a long moment, their eyes locked in a showdown. Matt's mouth firmed into a hard, determined line.

"I'm sure you will," he said in a steely tone that brooked no argument. "Because I'm spending the night with you."

Chapter Nine

"You're *what?*"

"Spending the night here with you." Matt's voice was as unyielding as the set of his jaw.

Of all the unmitigated nerve! Ali placed her hands on her hips and confronted him, her gray eyes blazing. "You most certainly are not!"

"If you insist on staying here with the windows wide open where anyone could just walk in, then I'm going to be here with you." His voice was maddeningly calm. "I'll sleep in the guest room."

Just who the heck did he think he was? "I don't recall inviting you to do any such thing," Ali said through gritted teeth.

Matt shrugged. "It's not safe for you to stay here alone with the house unlocked. If you won't swap houses for the night, then you leave me no choice."

"I don't need your protection," Ali protested.

"I disagree." Matt folded his arms stubbornly across his chest. "You may not mind endangering yourself and your property, but I'm not going to stand by and watch Robert's little sister deliberately put herself in harm's way."

Robert's little sister. So that was how he thought of her. The realization knocked all the wind out of her sails and made her stomach feel like she'd swallowed a lead cannonball.

Robert's little sister. Well, of course, she told herself, what else would she be to him? Her relationship to Robert was the only reason she and Matt knew each other, the only reason they were in business together, the only reason he'd spent the day with her and was here right now. It was the entire basis for their relationship.

She'd known that all along. So why did the words cut like a knife?

What did you think? she mentally chided herself. *That he cared for you and liked you and sought out your company just for the pleasure of it?*

Yes. If she were honest, that was exactly what she'd hoped.

"Well, this is my house and you're not staying," Ali told him, trying hard to imbue her voice with the force of her earlier conviction.

"Okay," Matt said evenly. "If you don't want me in the house, then I'll park in your driveway and sleep in my car."

It would serve him right, Ali thought hotly. But somehow the idea of Matt cramped in his car, trying to find a way to stretch his long frame in a comfortable position, upset her all the more.

Matt grabbed his jacket from the coat closet. "I'll be back in an hour or so."

Ali clenched her fists as the front door closed, fighting the urge to throw something after him. What an infuriating man!

She stormed angrily across the room and began tidying up the paint equipment with rapid, jerky motions. How dare he impose himself on her like this! Didn't he have any respect for her privacy, for her judgment, for her... her *personhood?*

Robert's sister, indeed! How dare he think of her as nothing except a relative of his former partner! She was a person in her own right—a person to be reckoned with, she thought indignantly. Not to mention a person whom he'd kissed.

Ali froze beside the folded stepladder, recalling the sparks that had flashed between them when she'd climbed down to find herself practically in his arms today. She was sure the attraction was mutual; the chemistry was too strong to be one-sided.

But of course Matt would never do anything about it. He was too logical, too rational. And too hung up on the misguided belief that he was some sort of surrogate big brother.

Not that she'd let him if he tried. Ali banged down the lid of a half-empty paint can with her fist.

Well, let him come back. She couldn't wait to give him a piece of her mind. She had a thing or two to tell that mule-headed, thick-skulled . . . *business partner.*

Her hand fell motionless at the thought. *I can't tell him off. I have to work with him.*

Deflated, Ali crossed the room and flopped onto the sheet-draped sofa in frustration. She'd never met such an exasperating man—a man who made her feel insulted and angry and completely unsettled. But because he held the final say over her work, she had to be nice to him.

If not nice, at least civil, she thought begrudgingly. Civil, calm, self-controlled and rational.

Ali heaved a sigh and kicked off her shoes. How was she going to manage that when her insides were twisted like a licorice stick? It didn't help that she was hot and tired and hungry and dirty.

A bath—that was just the ticket. A nice, hot bubble bath always lifted her spirits. A good long bath could make any situation more tolerable.

She rose from the sofa and quickly finished her cleanup tasks. Five minutes later, the tub was filling with warm water. She'd give herself the royal treatment, she decided, fetching her portable tape player and a pair of candles from her bedroom.

Soon the room was bathed in soft candlelight and gentle music. She'd take a whirlpool first, then add bubbles later, Ali decided.

She flipped the switch and the water began swirling around the tub. Peeling off her paint-splattered clothes, she stepped in and stretched out, luxuriating in the sensation of the warm water jets caressing her body on all sides. Ali closed her eyes—and immediately envisioned Matt's face.

His lips had looked so firm and demanding and hungry when he'd helped her down from the ladder, she thought dreamily. His breath had brushed her face and the faint scent of his shaving lotion had teased her nostrils. He'd wanted to kiss her; she'd seen the gleam of unmistakable intent in his eyes.

A surge of heat that had nothing to do with the water temperature began coursing through her, and she shifted restlessly in the water. One of the water jets now hit her side, exactly where Matt's hand had rested earlier.

What if his fingers had drifted slightly upward, just like the stream of water was doing now? It would have grazed the bottom of her breast. The thought caused a shiver to chase through her and Ali leaned back in the churning water, letting her imagination run as wild as the swirling whirlpools.

No! she thought suddenly. She switched off the jets and shot out of the water. Clutching her arms around herself, she stood in the tub, dripping and shivering in the cool air. She refused to allow herself to indulge in any more fantasies about Matt, she thought fiercely. It was foolish—beyond foolish.

Reckless. Dangerous.

She didn't want to get involved with Matt. It would never work out, and a failed romance with him would devastate all of her plans. Not to mention what it could do to her heart, she thought grimly. She was in too deep as it was.

Ali grabbed a jar of bubble bath and sat back down in the water. Turning on the faucet, she poured a generous amount of the scented soap into the stream of water, then leaned back as the tub filled with bubbles.

She lifted a handful of bubbles and absently let them sift through her fingers as her thoughts meandered over her limited romantic experience. None of her past involvements had lasted very long. She had a knack for picking the wrong type of man—either posturing macho types who fled when she spoke her mind or spineless wimps.

Matt didn't fit either category. He was independent, strong-willed and very much his own man. And as much as it infuriated her, she had to admit that it also pleased her in an odd, secret way. Matt was cut from a different cloth.

"Nonsense," she said aloud, reaching up to shut off the faucet. "He's just ten times as stubborn."

She rubbed herself down with a loofah, then leaned back in the tub, bending her leg and thoughtfully tracing one of the water jet outlets with her toe. She would do well to follow Matt's lead in one area, she decided; she needed to ignore their physical attraction and focus strictly on business. After the development was completed, she'd never have to see him again.

The thought left her depressed and restless, and she decided to get out of the tub. She sat up in the water, pushed her foot against the side of the tub, and accidently jammed her toe into the water jet.

She tried to pull it out, but it wouldn't budge. She tried again. She leaned forward, grasped her foot with her hands and yanked.

Nothing. She was stuck!

Panic rising in her chest, she gingerly felt her foot. The joint of her big toe was firmly wedged in the outlet. She squirmed and tugged and pulled for several long, uncomfortable minutes. Her efforts only succeeded in making her toe throb.

Oh, merciful heavens, what was she going to do?

"Ali?" Matt's voice came from the living room.

Matt—oh, no! Her heart thudded against her rib cage. She couldn't let him find her like this! She tugged at her toe again, creating a wrenching pain.

"Ow!" she yelped.

"Ali, are you all right? Where are you?"

You're stuck, she told herself grimly, *and you need help.*

But she was completely naked! Ali desperately looked around; the towels were out of reach and she'd left her robe in the bedroom. The only things at hand were a bar of soap and the bottle of bubble bath on the edge of the tub.

Ali grabbed the bubble bath and poured half the bottle into the water, then splashed furiously.

"I'm in here," she called over the music. "I'm stuck in the tub."

She heard footsteps in the hall. "You're *what?*"

"I'm stuck," she said, frustration raising her voice an octave. "My toe is jammed in the whirlpool. I've tried and tried, but I can't get it out."

The announcement was greeted with a silence so profound that Ali was afraid he'd turned around and left.

"I'm coming in," he finally said.

"Just a moment!" Ali sank low in the water, covering as much of herself as possible with a thick blanket of bubbles. She wrapped her arms across her breasts. "All right."

She watched Matt open the door cautiously and pause in the doorway as his eyes adjusted to the candlelight. Oh, mercy— she'd forgotten about the candles! Ali longed to just slide all the way under the water. What must he be thinking? She prayed he wouldn't suspect she'd staged some sort of seduction setup.

"I'm over here," she called out in a hoarse voice.

"I need to turn on a light so I can see you," Matt replied.

"No!" Ali gave her toe another yank, splashing water over the side of the tub. "I mean, I'm...I don't have on any...would you throw me a towel?"

Matt muttered an oath, then fumbled around until he found one.

Ali reached out and grabbed it. "Could you please turn around for a moment?"

Matt complied and Ali dragged the towel into the water, trying to cover herself with it. Maybe between the towel and the bubbles, she'd be able to maintain some semblance of decency.

"Okay," she finally said. Her mouth was so dry she could hardly swallow.

"I've got to turn on a light so I can see your toe," Matt told her.

The sudden glare made her wince. When she opened her eyes, Matt was staring at her. She met his gaze and quickly looked away. A wave of heat suffused her body despite the fact that the water was beginning to cool.

Matt knelt by the tub and gently touched her leg, sending shockwaves reverberating through her. She saw his Adam's apple bob as he swallowed. "The first thing we need to do is drain some of this water out so I can see your foot."

Ali hesitated, then nodded as she clutched the wet towel.

Matt pushed up his sleeves and plunged his hand into the water to open the drain. As the water receded, she slunk down further and further.

"Don't let out all the water—that's enough," she said abruptly as soon as her foot was in sight.

Matt turned his attention to her toe. "It's stuck, all right," he commented. "I'm going to get some ice."

A moment later he returned with a plastic sandwich bag filled with crushed ice. "This should make the swelling go down," he said, "but it won't be very comfortable."

"I'm not exactly lolling in luxury right now," Ali remarked.

Matt looked pointedly around the room and gave her a wry smile. "You could have fooled me," he said before wrapping the ice around her foot.

"Yikes!" Ali hollered. The shock of cold made her jump, causing the towel to slip. Ali struggled desperately to readjust it, hoping Matt hadn't noticed she'd just fully exposed her chest.

No such luck, Ali realized as she glanced at his face. When his eyes finally slid up to hers, they sparkled with amusement and . . . arousal. He quickly turned his attention back to her foot, and Ali clutched at the towel as if it were a life raft.

"We need to leave the ice on for a few minutes." He sat back on his heels and leaned an arm on the side of the tub. "While we're waiting, why don't you tell me just how this happened?"

"I was taking a bath," Ali said.

"I figured out that much," Matt said dryly. "What's with the candles and mood music?"

Ali tried to muster as much dignity as the situation would allow. "A woman's bath rituals are her own private business," she said haughtily, trying to hide her mortification with a show of bravado. "I was simply trying to unwind."

Matt readjusted the ice pack and lifted an eyebrow. "Uh-huh. And I suppose jamming your toe in a water outlet seemed like a good way to do that?"

"It was an accident," Ali snapped. "I suppose you find this all very amusing."

Matt's smile faded as he met her eyes. "Hey, I didn't mean to make fun of you. I'm sorry." His voice was sincere, his brown eyes warm. "I was just trying to lighten up the situation."

The last thing she'd expected from him was sensitivity; the second-to-last thing was an apology. She squirmed under the towel, unsure how to respond. "It's okay," she finally muttered. "I appreciate your help."

Matt returned his attention to her toe. "Why don't we see about getting this little guy free?"

He removed the ice pack, reached for the bubble bath and gently worked a generous amount of the slippery liquid around her foot. "Okay. Let your foot go completely limp. I'm going to try to work your toe out."

Clutching the towel, Ali leaned back, closed her eyes and tried to relax. It wasn't easy; she was far too aware of her state of undress, the sensuous setting and Matt's fingers on her feet.

His touch was surprisingly gentle—so gentle that Ali was startled when her toe suddenly slid out.

"Free at last," he said with a grin. He held her foot between his hands and studied her toe intently. "It's kind of red, but I think it's okay. How does it feel?"

Ali wiggled it cautiously. "A little tender, but otherwise it's fine."

Matt rubbed her toes. "This little piggy went to plumbing school, this little piggy stayed home . . ."

Ali splashed water at him, causing him to duck. "Having fun?" she asked.

"As a matter of fact, I am." He wiped the water off his face and ran his eyes across her. They lingered on her chest, causing Ali to tighten her grip on the towel. "It's not every day I get to rescue a beautiful damsel in distress—especially one who's completely naked, dripping wet and completely at my mercy."

Beautiful...naked...mercy. The teasing words hit Ali like waves, rocking her to the core. A shiver ran through her, a shiver of trepidation and anticipation and excitement.

"Thanks for the help. Now if you'll excuse me, I'd like to get out," she said.

Matt sat back on his heels and grinned at her. "By all means. Don't let me stop you."

"You need to leave the room," she told him pointedly.

"How do I know you won't get something else stuck the minute I turn my back?"

"I promise to call you if I do."

Matt rose to his feet. "All kidding aside," he said, his smile changing to a somber expression, "you shouldn't try to climb out alone. A bathtub is a dangerous, slippery place to experiment with putting weight on an injured foot. And all that bubble bath in the water doesn't help the situation."

Ali rearranged the wet towel over herself as best she could. "If you think I'm going to stand up stark naked in front of you, you need to think again," she said stiffly.

"I'll close my eyes," Matt said. He turned and rummaged in the linen closet opposite the tub. Withdrawing an enormous pink towel, he unfolded it and draped it over his arm. "I'll even turn out the light."

He reached over and flipped the switch, plunging the room back into candlelit intimacy. "I won't touch you. I'll just hold out my hands, and you can use them to steady yourself."

Hugging her wet towel with one hand, Ali lifted her foot and rubbed it. The toe throbbed and her arch had a painful cramp—no doubt the result of having been suspended in such an awkward position for so long.

Matt was right, Ali thought reluctantly, it wasn't a good idea for her to climb out of the tub alone. Especially considering her track record for calamities.

She looked up at him, her heart pounding in her throat. "Do you promise to keep your eyes closed?" she asked.

Matt held up two fingers. "Scout's honor."

"How do I know you were ever a Scout?" she queried suspiciously.

"You'll just have to trust me."

The sensuous strains of a steamy love ballad reverberated in the small room. A tremor raced through Ali. She chose to attribute it the increasingly chilly temperature of the water.

Whatever it took, she had to get out of that bathtub. And it looked like it was going to take Matt's help.

Ali swallowed hard. "All right," she relented. "Close your eyes."

Matt stepped up to the tub and extended his hands. Satisfied that his eyes were shut, Ali clutched the wet towel with one hand and grabbed his arm with the other. She couldn't stand this way, she realized; she would have to drop the towel.

She tentatively reached out her other hand and clutched his steely forearm. Her throat constricted at the feel of his brawny muscle. Hesitantly, she pulled herself out of the water and to her feet.

She took a deep breath, stepped out of the tub…and lurched against his chest.

His arm encircled her, his hand resting on her bare back just above her buttocks. She froze, not daring to back away from him for fear of exposing herself. His chest was hard and warm, and she could feel his heart pound beneath the smooth cotton of his shirt.

He somehow arranged the dry towel around her back. Her skin tingled with a new, heightened sensitivity as he gently dried her, sliding the terry cloth across her shoulder blades, past her waist and down her hips. She was acutely aware that the front of her, the part pressed against his shirt and faded jeans, was as naked as the day she was born. The knowledge both thrilled and terrified her.

Ali looked up at him in the flickering candlelight, her heart in her throat. His eyes were open now, open and dark and hungry. She felt his arms tighten around her and a deep ache began to throb within her.

"You're trembling," he whispered. "Are you cold?"

She was too hot to feel cold. Ali wordlessly shook her head, her breath catching in her throat.

His eyes searched hers in the candlelight. Her arms stretched up around his neck, answering his unspoken question, and the next thing she knew, his mouth covered hers.

His lips brushed hers gently, then retreated and advanced again, finally settling firmly on her mouth in a demanding kiss. He pulled back and nibbled her bottom lip, then fully claimed her mouth once more, this time ravishing it with his tongue. The kiss sent her spiraling into a blurred world of sweet, hot yearning. Her fingers ran along the muscled cords of his neck, across the steely ridge of his shoulder, down the solid planes of his back. She arched against him, wanting more.

"Ali, honey," he breathed, his fingers threading in her hair.

He wound his other arm around her and deepened the kiss. The world narrowed to nothing but Matt, to nothing but the hard warmth of his body, the delicious slide of his lips, the intoxicating scent that was his alone. She moved against him, mindless of where they were and what she wasn't wearing.

She was gasping for breath when he abruptly set her from him.

"I'd better go," he said in a husky voice.

Her hand fell from his shoulder as he bent and retrieved the towel from the floor. As if from a distance, her passion-fogged senses registered surprise that it had fallen. She stood motionless, dazed by desire, as he gently wrapped it around her.

"Under the circumstances, I'd better sleep in my car tonight." His voice was a thick, ragged growl.

The candles flickered as he opened and closed the bathroom door. Ali stood still as a statue long minutes after he'd gone, her head swimming, her heart aching, her toe forgotten.

Chapter Ten

Hattie furrowed her brow as she entered Matt's office early Monday morning. "You don't look so good. Are you coming down with something?"

"I'm fine," Matt muttered, running a hand down his face as he looked up from the paperwork on his desk. "Just a little beat, that's all."

Hattie cast a keen eye over him as she gathered up the papers from his Out box. "Most folks rest on the weekend. Judging from the amount of paperwork here, you spent at least half of it at the office." She shot him a disapproving look. "All work and no play is no good for anyone. You need more of a personal life, Matt."

Matt eyed her in exasperation and bit back a sharp retort. "I'm doing just fine, thank you." Pretending to return his attention to the papers on his desk, he adopted a businesslike tone. "I'd-like to see the updated completion schedule as soon as possible."

"I'll take care of it." Hattie hesitated at the door. "Can I bring you an aspirin or anything?"

"No. I told you I'm fine," he snapped.

"If this is fine, I'd hate to see you have a bad day." Hattie shook her head as she closed the door behind her.

Matt pushed back his chair and sighed. The truth was, he felt terrible. It was no wonder—he'd hardly slept all weekend. He'd spent Saturday night in his car in Ali's driveway, fighting the urge to march back into her house and take her in his arms. He'd lain awake till dawn and had pulled a muscle in his neck trying to stretch out in his car.

He'd spent the whole day at the office yesterday trying to distract himself with work, taking twice as long as usual to accomplish anything because his thoughts kept turning to Ali. He'd gone on a five-mile run in the evening, but despite his best efforts to exhaust himself, he'd spent the entire night tossing and turning, haunted by thoughts of her. He'd picked up the phone to call her half a dozen times, only to put it back in its cradle.

Matt massaged his temple, where a dull ache was gaining momentum. Maybe he'd lost his mind. Why else would he have crushed her to him like that and kissed her until he couldn't see straight?

While she was stark naked, yet!

And why else was he behaving like a besotted schoolboy with a first crush, unable to think about anything but Ali's laugh and Ali's face and Ali's luscious, lovely curves?

The thought sent a fresh ripple of desire coursing through his body. Jamming his hands into his pockets, he strode to the window and gazed out at the sun-dappled woods. Tender leaves were sprouting from gray oak branches and tight blossoms were unfurling on the redbud trees. The scenery was green and hopeful and it quickened something inside him, some part he'd thought was dead and buried.

If I didn't know better, I'd think I was lovesick.

The thought startled Matt. Who said anything about love? He'd tried the love route, and it wasn't for him.

He just had a bad case of spring fever, that was all, and he was projecting his feelings onto Ali.

Ali. Matt rubbed his chin thoughtfully and watched a mockingbird light on the slender twig of a persimmon tree.

The woman was a mass of contradictions. How could one person be so endearing and so aggravating at the same time? There were times when she seemed to embody every fantasy he'd ever had about a woman. Visions of Ali flashed through his mind—Ali dancing at the wedding, looking like an angel in that billowing pink dress; Ali perched on the ladder, smiling down at him; Ali gazing up at him, her eyes dark with desire, her lips moist and parted and begging to be kissed.

Matt gnawed his lower lip. Of course, there was also Ali the human whirlwind, he reminded himself—creating one bizarre incident after another, disrupting his business, knocking the breath out of him literally and figuratively. She was not only befuddling his life, now she was confusing his thoughts, as well.

What kind of future could a man have with a woman like that?

What kind of future could he have without her? Matt muttered an oath, wanting her to the point of distraction. He had half a mind to throw caution to the wind, follow his urges and sort it all out later.

Matt's thoughts were interrupted by a knock on his door. "Come in," he called gruffly.

Speak of the devil. Ali stood in the doorway, wearing some kind of Indian motif skirt that fell to midcalf. Her hair was pulled back from her face and silver Indian-style earrings sparkled at her ears. Another woman might look silly in that getup, but Ali looked stylish and artsy and fresh.

His heart turned over. With the slightest provocation, he'd pull her into his arms and kiss her halfway into tomorrow.

She stood framed in the doorway for a moment, hesitating, then closed the door behind her. "I think we should talk," she said.

Matt strode to his desk, trying to act like his heart wasn't pounding like a roofing carpenter's hammer, and stood behind his chair. "What about?"

"About what happened Saturday."

Matt swallowed hard. Had she been replaying it in her mind like he had? Had it affected her like it affected him? Were her insides quivering like a piece of wood under a buzz saw, longing to take up where they'd left off? He was shocked at how desperately he hoped it was so.

"What about it?" he asked, his voice a shade deeper than usual.

Ali crossed the room and seated herself primly on the edge of an armchair across from his desk. "It was an unfortunate incident." She folded her hands in her lap and gazed down at them. "It was an unusual situation and we both reacted unusually to its...unusualness. I think we should forget about it. I'm sorry it happened and I'd like to put it behind us." She finished the statement in a rush of words, as if she were reciting a rehearsed speech, then glanced up at him from beneath her lashes.

Matt abruptly turned back to the window. He felt like she'd just walloped him in the stomach, but he'd be darned if he let her know it.

"An unfortunate incident." She made kissing him sound as enjoyable as a root canal! Matt narrowed his eyes as he stared out the window and was glad when anger started to mercifully flow through him, at least partially filling the hole her words had just blasted.

She was absolutely right, of course. Getting involved with her would be completely irrational, and rational behavior was the guiding principle of his life. He'd had a terrible lapse in judgment. He knew better than to even think of a relationship with anyone as erratic and unpredictable as Ali.

She wished it had never happened, did she? Well, that went double for him!

"It was nothing," he retorted. His hand cut through the air in a dismissive gesture. "It's already forgotten." Matt strode to his desk and seated himself behind it, picking up a stack of papers. "It's never a good idea to mix business and pleasure anyway."

"No, it's not. And we're just too different."

"Like oil and water," he agreed.

From the corner of his eye, he thought he saw her posture droop. He couldn't be sure, because she immediately pulled her shoulders back and raised her head. Her earrings jingled faintly as she lifted her chin. "Fine. I'm glad you agree." She rose to her feet, her voice brisk and businesslike. "The samples I was waiting on arrived over the weekend. When you get time, I'd like to show you the boards."

Matt nodded, busily straightening the papers on his desk into three neat, precise stacks. "I've got some important things to finish up here, and then I've got some appointments." His tone was stiff and formal. "I'll try to make time tomorrow or the next day."

Matt felt the heat of her eyes on him and glanced up. She stood by the chair, twirling the strap of her purse, and for just a moment she seemed to have lost her starch. She looked away, but not before he glimpsed her eyes, which held the look of a wounded deer.

"Fine," she murmured, turning and closing the door softly behind her.

The sight put a damper on his anger but somehow heightened his distress. *She's disappointed that I'm not eager to see her work.* He pulled three paper clips from his desk and fastened them in careful, identical corners on each stack of paper, then consolidated them into one precise pile, carefully aligning all four edges. It was a sure sign he was agitated; the more upset he was, the more precise he became. It soothed him to bring order to his immediate surroundings when his emotions were in chaos.

Well, so what? he asked himself, trying to recapture some of his earlier indignation. Why should he pretend to be jumping up and down with eagerness to see her designs? He'd told her at the outset that he didn't need an interior designer, but she'd insisted on imposing her services on him anyway. Besides, if she were to get the idea that her contributions were valuable, she'd probably want to stay on and continue to work at the firm after the project was completed.

So why did he feel like such a heel? After all, she'd been the one who'd bruised his ego.

More than bruised, he thought, unconsciously rubbing his chest—completely deflated. He felt lower than the drainpipe on a septic system.

Well, it served him right for thinking about her in terms he never should have pursued. Hadn't he known from the start that she was nothing but trouble?

Chapter Eleven

"So how are things at work?" Susan asked, handing Ali a glass of iced tea.

Ali leaned against Susan's kitchen counter and took a sip, watching her friend peer through the window in the oven door. "Okay, I guess. Mmm . . . Is that apple pie?"

Susan straightened and eyed her keenly. "Don't try to change the subject. What do you mean, 'okay'? Didn't you show Matt your designs last week?"

Ali set her glass on the countertop and sighed. When she'd accepted Susan's dinner invitation, she'd hoped to get her mind off Matt for an evening. Heaven only knew she needed a reprieve from the thoughts of him that hounded her at home as well as work.

Her newly painted walls were a constant reminder. She avoided her own living room, she took showers instead of baths and she'd removed the picnic quilt from her bedroom. She couldn't seem to escape him even in sleep. Not that her restless, all-night thrashing actually counted as sleep.

The last thing she wanted to do right now was talk about Matt, but she knew Susan, and she knew her friend wouldn't be diverted from the topic until her curiosity was satisfied. "I showed Matt the designs, but he didn't respond exactly like I'd envisioned."

Susan pulled a blue oven mitt off a hook by the stove and fitted it on her hand. "Didn't he like them? What did he say?"

"He said they were fine."

Susan's brow knit in confusion. "So what's the problem?"

Have you got three hours to listen to a sob story? Ali decided to confine her remarks to work. "He said 'fine'—not 'good,' not 'creative,' just 'fine'! I've spent more time and effort on this than on any project in my career, and all the man can say is 'fine'!" Ali's voice vibrated with frustration. "He barely looked at them. He spent more time going over the cost estimates than looking at the boards." Ali slapped her hand on the countertop. "I swear, Susan, he's the most obstinate, pig-headed, frustrating man I've ever had to deal with!"

Susan eyed her with amusement. "Sounds to me like you've got it bad."

"Got what bad?"

"A case for Matt."

"The only case I'd like to have for that man would be filled with dynamite."

"So there's nothing going on between the two of you?"

Ali hesitated and glanced at Susan. Her friend knew her too well for her to bluff her way out of answering. Besides, Ali needed to talk to someone. The problem was she dreaded putting her feelings into words; if she left them unspoken, unexamined, unnamed, maybe she wouldn't have to address them.

Who am I trying to kid?

"No. Yes—no!" Ali ran a hand through her hair and began pacing the kitchen. "There's a physical attraction between us, but we're too different for anything serious to develop."

"Opposites can do more than just attract, Ali. Sometimes they're perfect for balancing each other out." Susan eyed her curiously. "So tell me, have you done anything about this attraction?"

"No. Yes—no!" Ali heaved a forceful sigh. "We've kissed, but he agrees with me that it was a mistake."

Susan held up an oven-mitted hand. "Wait a minute. Let me get this straight. You told him it was a mistake?" At Ali's nod, Susan shook her head in disbelief. "Why on earth did you do that if you care for the guy?"

Ali stared down at her fingers. "The circumstances were kind of . . . unusual, and we got a little carried away. I didn't want him avoiding me at work, so I tried to smooth things over."

Susan shook her head. "I don't understand you, Ali. You're obviously nuts about him. Why didn't you try to parlay the 'unusual circumstances' into a relationship?"

Ali seated herself on a bar stool by the counter. "I need a man who believes in me, who has confidence in my judgment. I want someone who feels like I'm an equal, not a liability." She exhaled harshly. "Besides, Matt's told me he doesn't ever want to get married again, and I'm not interested in a casual affair. I want the full-meal deal—commitment, marriage, children. The only thing he's in the market for relationshipwise is a fast-food snack."

Susan's forehead creased in a worried frown. "In light of all this, I guess you won't be pleased with who else is coming to dinner tonight."

Ali stared at her friend. "You didn't."

Susan shrugged sheepishly. "Afraid I did." Susan gazed out the window. "And they're coming up the walk now."

"Oh, no!" Ali wailed just as a door opened in the foyer.

"Hello!" called Hank.

"Something sure smells delicious," said an unmistakably familiar male voice. Ali's heart pounded traitorously as the two men entered the kitchen.

Matt froze, his smile fading. She forced a smile. "Hello, Matt."

"Ali." He gave her a polite nod, his expression shuttered. "It's a surprise to see you here."

I'll bet. Otherwise you wouldn't have come. "I didn't expect to see you, either."

She quickly turned her attention to Hank, hoping to hide the blush she knew was staining her face. "You look great, Hank." She gave him a warm hug. "Marriage must agree with you."

"Thanks. I've got no complaints." The lanky man gave his wife a tender kiss accompanied by such an unabashedly adoring gaze that Ali had to look away. To her consternation, Matt was directly in her line of vision.

He quickly averted his eyes, his gaze settling on the wide window in the breakfast room. It overlooked a long wooden deck, which in turn overlooked a tree-lined pond. Weeping willows, mimosas, poplars and redbuds were sending out tender green shoots, their tiny leaves bright against a dense stand of dark cedars.

"What a terrific view!" Matt remarked, moving toward the window.

"Isn't it?" Susan replied with a smile. "The land was Hank's grandfather's. The weather's so pretty tonight that I thought we'd eat outdoors where we can enjoy it. Hank is going to throw some steaks on the grill."

"Hey, Matt, want to try out my new rod and reel while I'm heating up the coals? The pond is stocked with some good-size perch and catfish."

"That sounds great," Matt agreed.

Hank turned to Ali. "How about you, Ali? I can fix you up with a line, too, if you like."

"I'll stay here and help Susan," she demurred.

Susan shook her head. "Nonsense! I've got everything under control. Besides, I remember how much you loved fishing when we were kids. Go for it!" She gave Ali a meaningful look and a little push toward the back door.

Ali found herself following Matt and Hank down the sloping lawn to a wooden storage shed, silently fuming about her friend's none-too-subtle matchmaking techniques. She stood awkwardly outside the little building with Matt as Hank rummaged inside.

Ali pretended a keen interest in a flowering dogwood and Matt silently studied the pond as tension coiled between them.

She was vainly searching her mind for an excuse to back out of the outing when Hank emerged and presented each of them with a rod and reel.

Ali eyed the shiny equipment dubiously. "Gee, Hank, I've never used anything this high tech. Maybe I should just go back inside and visit with Susan."

"This is easier to use than a bamboo pole once you get the hang of it. Matt can show you everything you need to know." Hank closed the door to the shed with a bang. "The fish were biting under that big willow last night," he said, pointing to a spot halfway around the pond. "I caught two sun perch and a crappie."

"Sounds like a good spot. Thanks, Hank," Matt replied.

Hank waved his hand and headed back toward the house. Matt turned to Ali. "Ready?"

Ali hesitated, then nodded. She couldn't avoid him forever; after all, she did have to work with him, and they needed to get comfortable again in each other's company. Maybe a fishing expedition would help normalize their relationship.

She imitated the way Matt shouldered his rod and reel and trudged along beside him, searching for something to say.

"It's beautiful here," she commented. The topic had already been covered, but nothing else came to mind and she was desperate to break the silence. "I knew Hank lived in the country, but I didn't expect anything like his."

Matt nodded. "It's nice—and so's this gear. The winner of last year's striper tournament at Lake Texoma used a rig just like the one you're carrying."

"Oh," Ali said. She felt as awkward and unsure as a schoolgirl. "Do you want to trade?"

Matt's face softened into a grin. "No. This one's just as nice. But thanks for the offer."

They fell into another silence as they followed a path around the pond. "It sounds like you know a lot about fishing," Ali remarked.

Matt shrugged. "I don't get much of chance to enjoy the sport, but I've always loved it."

Ali looked at him in surprise. "I never would have guessed that of you."

Matt slowly raised an eyebrow. "Why not?"

Ali lifted her shoulders. "I don't know. It's not the sort of thing I thought you'd do." She paused to readjust her grip on the pole and Matt stopped, too, his brown eyes drinking her in. She wasn't dressed in anything fancy, just faded jeans and a chambray shirt, but she looked good enough to eat. It took all of his considerable willpower to keep from pulling her into his arms and kissing her senseless. He knew just how she liked it—slow and soft at first, then deepening and building, growing harder and faster until his lips were doing what the rest of him longed to do: claim full and complete possession.

She was looking at him and he realized the conversational ball was in his court. He forced his thoughts back to the present. "Why did you think I wouldn't like to fish?"

"It's not predictable. You can't control whether the fish bite or not."

Matt cast her a sidelong glance and resumed walking. Did she really see him as such a control freak? He didn't find the image at all flattering.

He started to say as much, then bit back his retort. Denying it would only prove her point, he thought reluctantly. She'd probably think he was trying to control her opinion of him.

All the same, her comment needled him like a pine branch. So she thought he was tense and stuffy, did she? Was that why she didn't want to get romantically involved—she thought he was too controlling? Matt clenched his teeth together, tightening his jaw. Well, from now on, by golly, he'd make a point of showing her just how easygoing and open-minded he could be.

He stopped beside a large willow. "This looks like the spot."

Ali came up beside him, breathing hard, and brushed a curl from her forehead. "Oh, it's beautiful."

You certainly are. He forced himself to turn his eyes away from her and grunted agreement, trying to focus on the tranquil pond. If Ali didn't have him in such a state of—what? edginess? irritation? *arousal?*—he would have found the setting exceedingly peaceful. A chorus of tree frogs and crickets had begun an evening serenade, and the air smelled fresh and earthy.

Matt set down his fishing rod and turned to Ali. She was studying her fishing gear with a puzzled frown.

"Would you like some help?"

"Yes," she said gratefully.

"I'll get your line unwound and show you how to cast," Matt offered. He was conscious of Ali's eyes on him as he rolled up the sleeves of his denim shirt. He took the rod from her and deftly unwrapped the line, noting that it was already set with a bright green lure hiding a cloverleaf of four hooks.

"Looks like a giant bug," Ali remarked.

"Let's see if the fish think so, too," Matt said. "I'll cast it out and you can reel it in."

Matt lifted the rod, swung it back and tossed the line out to the middle of the pond. "Here," he said, handing it to Ali. He stepped behind her and placed his hands over hers, inadvertently inhaling the soft scent of her hair. She brushed against him as she adjusted her stance, and his body immediately responded. "Hold it like this, and reel it in nice and steady," he said, trying to reel in his thoughts as well. "Keep the line taut and occasionally give it a little jerk."

"Why do you do that?" Ali asked. She was involved in her own struggle to focus on fishing. Why, oh, why, did this impossible man have the power to turn her joints to jelly? She was all too aware that Matt's chest was pressed against her back, and it was all she could do to keep from leaning back against him. Her face felt flushed and her hands were trembling.

"To trick the fish," Matt said. He tugged sharply on the line to demonstrate. "You try it."

Ali wound the reel as he'd shown her, then gave it a quick pull. The line barely moved on the water.

"You have to pull it harder," Matt said. "Get the line good and tight, then give it a solid pop."

Her brow furrowed in concentration, Ali cranked the reel, then gave a hard tug. The lure came flying out of the water, directly at her face.

She wasn't sure if the yell that rang in her ears came from her or Matt. She felt his arm reach up protectively as she ducked and closed her eyes.

When she opened them, the bug was perched on Matt's forearm.

"Oh, Matt! Are you all right?"

Matt gingerly fingered the lure, buying time to compose himself before he replied. Ali had nearly nailed herself in the face with the four-way hook and his heart was still in his throat. If anything had happened to her, he'd never have been able to forgive himself. "I'd be a lot better if I didn't have this creature stuck on my arm," he said gruffly. "Would you see if you can get it off?"

Ali gently took his arm, making it impossible for his heart rate to return to normal. Her hands were cool on his skin, and Matt found himself staring at her soft, fair fingers, struck by the way they contrasted with the hard tan of his forearm, remembering how they had played over his back when he'd kissed her. Those hands had driven him crazy, were driving him crazy now.

She gingerly touched the bug, creating a sharp bite of pain that made Matt wince.

"Matt, I'm so sorry," she murmured, her eyes large with worry. "Two of the hooks are imbedded in your skin."

At least the pain was a distraction from his thoughts. "Well, see if you can work them out."

Couldn't this woman do anything without creating some sort of crisis? She'd come close to putting her eye out with the lure. Didn't she have the foggiest idea how to take care of herself?

He opened his mouth, ready to launch into a safety lecture, then shut it abruptly.

Whoa, boy. You're trying to do away with the stuffed-shirt image, remember? If he really wanted to change her opinion of him, this was a perfect opportunity. A little calm understanding could go a long way.

He'd been looking away, not trusting himself to watch her, but now he glanced down. Her head was bent over his arm, her hair falling against her cheeks in a mass of curls as unruly as the woman herself.

"The hooks have barbs on the ends of them. I think we'd better get you to a doctor." Ali released his arm and looked up at him, her eyes filled with concern and remorse. "Matt, I'm so sorry."

The sight of her distress did something funny to Matt's chest. "Hey, it was an accident, that's all. It's my fault for sticking my arm out there."

"I would have been hit in the face if you hadn't."

He reached out and touched her cheek. "It's not worth getting all upset over. I'm fine." Her skin was soft and warm, and his finger lingered.

Matt lowered his gaze to her full, ripe lips. They were so tempting, so incredibly tempting. It would be so easy to just lean down and kiss her. Her lips were parted, and the look in her eyes was an open invitation . . .

Put a lid on it, Jordan. You don't want to create another "unfortunate incident."

The memory of her words stung worse than the hooks in his skin. The lady had made it clear his attentions weren't welcome, he reminded himself. Never mind that she'd instigated the whole thing in the first place, never mind that the electricity crackling between them had enough voltage to light up the entire town for a month, never mind that her face was tilted up and her eyes were half closed and she looked for all the world like a woman dying to be kissed. She'd said they should call it off, so the next move had to be hers.

"Let's go see about getting this thing off me," Matt said abruptly. He picked up her fishing rod and expertly reeled in the loose line. "I'll carry this one. I seem to have developed an attachment to it."

She laughed at the joke and walked beside him back to the house, where they found Hank and Susan tending a smoking charcoal grill on the deck.

"Looks like you caught a big one!" Hank said to Matt, his face creased in an enormous grin.

"Something like that," Matt responded. "Jerked the line a little too fast."

Ali's eyebrows flew up in surprise. He wasn't going to tell them the accident was her fault! The small kindness touched her heart. She'd been braced for a round of ribbing and she was immensely relieved to be spared the unwelcome attention. She felt so responsible for Matt's predicament that she could barely look him in the eye as it was.

"Ali thinks I need to see a doctor," he said. "Take a look and see what you think."

Hank examined Matt's arm. "If you were a catfish, we'd be heating up the frying pan," he chortled.

Susan rolled her eyes. "You won't get a straight answer out of Hank. Better let me take a look." She studied Matt's arm for a moment. When she glanced up, her expression was serious. "Ali's right. This needs medical attention."

Matt heaved a resigned sigh and turned to Ali. "Well, I guess you'd better drive me to the emergency room."

To his surprise, Ali's face drained of color.

"There's a new all-night clinic across from the shopping center," Susan suggested quickly.

"Let's try there," Ali said.

Matt nodded, puzzled. For some reason that Susan seemed to understand, Ali wanted to avoid the hospital. "Anyplace where someone can get this thing off my arm is fine with me." He turned to Susan. "Do you have some scissors? I don't want to take any more of Hank's gear with me than I have to."

"Gee, Matt, I'd hate to cut a perfectly good line," Hank teased.

Hank kept up a steady stream of wisecracks as Susan snipped the line, and Matt was relieved when he and Ali finally headed outdoors to her tiny red sports car.

"I think you'd better drive," he said as Ali circled to the right side of the vehicle.

"I'm planning to." She climbed in, reached across the seat and unlocked the left door, pushing it open from the inside. Matt blinked hard as he looked through the door.

"What the heck . . ." he sputtered.

"You're probably wondering why the steering wheel is on the right side."

"The question crossed my mind."

"Well, it's a foreign car."

Matt reluctantly lowered himself into the car, folding his long frame onto the cramped seat. "I don't know if you've noticed, Ali, but there are lots of foreign cars on the road, and the vast majority of them manage to have their steering wheels located on the right side."

"You mean the left," Ali said, buckling her seatbelt.

"Right." Matt gave his head a shake and slammed the door shut. "I mean, correct." How did she manage to confuse him so easily? He prided himself on his clearheaded thinking. "So how did you happen to buy a car with the steering wheel on the wrong side?"

Ali started the engine. "A client inherited it from a relative in England and he sold it to me for just the shipping costs."

Matt's body tensed from the soles of his shoes to the ends of his hair as she pulled out of the driveway. He gazed warily out the window. "Is this legal?"

"Sure." Ali gave him a sidelong smile. "Don't worry, you'll get used to it after a while. And it has its advantages. Parallel parking is a whole lot easier."

Parallel parking didn't top his current list of concerns.

Ali accelerated as she pulled out onto the highway and glanced over at him. "I warned you that you wouldn't like my car."

Matt scowled, remembering her comment about the former boyfriend. He didn't like being lumped into the same callous mold as an old boyfriend—especially since he'd just made up his mind to show her he wasn't as rigid and stuffy as she thought.

Come to think of it, he didn't like the idea of an old boyfriend, period.

"I didn't say I didn't like it," Matt said cautiously. "It just takes some getting used to, that's all."

A car going the opposite direction whizzed by his window, causing Matt to wince and tighten his grip on the seat. He felt like a sitting duck, riding powerless in what should be the driver's seat.

Which just about summed up his feelings about their whole relationship.

He decided to turn his attention away from the window and focus completely on her. "I got the distinct impression you didn't want to go to the hospital."

The silence stretched out so long Matt began to think she wasn't going to reply. "I've got kind of a phobia about it," she finally confessed.

"Is there a reason?"

"Yes." She expelled a deep sigh. "My mother died there. She was in and out for the last six months of her life, enduring all sorts of cancer treatments. All of them made her weak and ill, and none of them helped."

"I'm sorry," Matt said quietly. "That must have been terrible."

The depth of concern in Matt's voice made her cast a glance at him. He was watching her intently, his eyes warm and somber in the light of the passing street lamps. She never talked about her mother's death—hadn't spoken of it in at least three years, in fact—but she suddenly found herself wanting to.

"Mom hated going to the hospital. Her last wish was to die at home." Ali turned into a parking lot where a large sign proclaimed Family Medical Center. Steering into a parking slot, she shut off the engine and turned to Matt. "One night when Robert was out of town, she had a really bad spell. I took her to the hospital, thinking it would be like all the other times—that she'd get stabilized and released."

Ali could barely speak around the lump in her throat. "But she died," she said in a voice scarcely more than a whisper. Ali stared at her fingers in her lap. "I felt like I let her down. After she died, I started getting panic attacks every time I'd drive by the place. I left town soon afterward. It's one of the reasons I stayed away from Hillsboro."

"Oh, honey—I had no idea," Matt said softly. He reached out and touched her cheek. The caress was so warm and reassuring, his voice so caring, that Ali squeezed her eyes shut, trying to hold back the flood of tears that threatened to erupt at the tender gesture. She had been holding back her emotions for so long—emotions about her mother, emotions about Robert . . . emotions about Matt.

Especially about Matt. Her mother and Robert were gone; Matt was here—alive, compelling, touchable.

And she loved him. Ali drew in a ragged breath and stared out the windshield. She'd tried to deny it, tried not to think about it, tried to convince herself that if she didn't name it, didn't call it love, it wouldn't be real—that she could just walk away from him unscathed when the project was finished.

But she loved him. And she knew, as she looked at him in the glow of the red neon sign, that no amount of denial would change the fact. Just as she knew that no amount of wishing would ever make a relationship between a control freak like Matt and an independent spirit like herself work for any amount of time.

"Sounds like you did what you thought was best for your mom at the time. How could that be letting her down?" Matt asked softly.

Ali shrugged. "I should have known how close she was to the end. I'm sure there were some signs I missed." Ali glanced at him then looked away, her gaze settling on her fingers twisted together in her lap. "Let's face it, Matt, I'm always screwing things up—especially for people I care about. Just look at your arm."

Matt's heart began to trip wildly as he stared at her. Had she just admitted she cared for him? Her comment was a slip of the tongue; maybe it meant nothing. On the other hand, maybe it meant everything.

What the heck did he hope it meant? Better stick with a safe topic until he could figure things out.

Matt gestured to his arm. "This could have happened to anyone. You were just trying to follow my instructions."

"What about the Heimlich manuever? Or when I hit you with the truck door? Or the time I backed into you when you were bringing me firewood?" Ali sighed deeply and gazed out at the deserted parking lot. "It's no wonder you don't have any confidence in my abilities as an interior designer."

"Whoa, there." Matt slid his hand under her hair, fervently wishing he had the use of both arms so he could gather her to him. He settled for rubbing her neck. "Aren't you jumping to conclusions? All of those incidents were all at least fifty percent my fault. And as for your abilities as an interior designer—I was really impressed with the designs you showed me."

Her eyes were clouded with doubt. "You sure didn't act like it. And when I asked if I could go ahead and order the materials, you told me to wait."

Matt squirmed on the seat. "I don't show my feelings very easily," he mumbled.

How could he tell her the real reason—that he'd been hurt over her rejection, angry that she'd so casually dismissed an attraction as strong as the pull of gravity? His reaction had had nothing to do with her designs. The truth was, he'd thought her designs were terrific. He still wasn't sure they'd sell, but they looked wonderful.

Tell her, his heart urged.

"Now that I've had time to think it over, I want you to proceed," he told her. "I'll be out of town at a convention for the next two weeks, but you can go ahead and get started. Order the materials, hire the subcontractors and schedule the work. Hattie can give you the names of the subs we usually use." He slid his hand up her neck into her hair, sifting the silken strands through his fingers. "I thought your designs were great, Ali. You're very talented."

Her smile reminded him of a kid at Christmas. Something stirred inside him, something he'd forgotten he could feel.

"Thanks, Matt," Ali said, leaning over and impulsively giving him a hug.

Matt's hand tightened in her hair as he inhaled her soft, womanly scent. She turned her face toward him and the next thing he knew, his mouth covered hers, all resolve forgotten. He didn't know who had made the first move and he didn't care. All that mattered were her lips, soft and giving and sweet, as urgently needy as his own.

She moaned and moved toward him, raising up and over the gearshift. He reached to pull her to him and was jabbed by a stabbing pain.

"Ow!"

"Oh, no!" Ali's hand flew to her mouth in horror. "Matt, I'm so sorry!"

Matt gritted his teeth. "It's nothing." She'd hit the lure, jamming the hooks deeper into his skin, but he was far more concerned with her feelings than his own physical discomfort. He cradled his arm as he opened the door. "Let's go get this thing taken off so we can get back to Hank and Susan's."

He'd better watch out, he warned himself. The hooks Ali was getting into him weren't as superficial as the ones on his arm.

Chapter Twelve

Hattie looked up from her typewriter and smiled as Matt strode into the office two weeks later. "Welcome back! How was the convention?"

Matt shrugged. "Okay, I guess. I learned quite a bit—lots of new building materials are coming on the market. How are things here?" Matt picked up the mail that had accumulated during his absence and sifted through it as he headed to his private office.

Hattie rose and marched along behind him. "Never better! Ali's doing a terrific job."

Matt nodded, his eyes still on the mail. "I swung by the job site before I came in this morning. Looks like things are moving along." Matt rounded his desk and eased himself into the tall leather chair as he pulled a bill out of an envelope. "The painting and paperhanging are progressing nicely."

"The interiors are beautiful, aren't they?" Hattie prodded. "Ali's handled it all herself, and she's ahead of schedule. I tell you, that gal is really something."

Matt glanced up at her and smiled in amusement. Her efforts to sell him on Ali were completely transparent. It seemed to be a community effort lately; Hattie, Hank and Susan—and now that he thought back on it, even Robert—had all tried to pair him off with Ali.

Could it be that they'd all been right?

During the time he'd been gone, he'd had lots of time to think, and all he could think about was a pair of wide gray eyes, a smile that should be selling toothpaste and a body that needed a Dangerous Curves warning sign attached to it.

Thinking of Ali now, he restlessly drummed his fingers on the desk and stared out the window. The woods were no longer just a promise of spring, but the lush fulfillment. The leaves were new and shiny and perfectly formed, not yet battered by wind or spotted by drought. The scene was a testimonial to fresh starts and new beginnings, and gazing at it made him long for one of his own.

With Ali? A jolt of adrenaline surged through him at the thought.

Impossible.

Or was it? All he knew for sure was that she made his heart unfurl like an oak leaf in the sun and that he couldn't get her off his mind. He'd always been a man of action, and it made no sense for him to just sit around and pine after her. He had to *do* something. As irrational as it seemed at first blush, it was beginning to look like the only logical course of action was to pursue her and see what happened.

Matt realized Hattie was still standing in front of his desk expectantly. "The houses are turning out better than I thought they would," he agreed noncommittally. He opened his calendar and scanned the entries, anxious to get the day's pressing business out of the way so he could go see Ali. "Is anything going on today that I need to know about?"

Hattie nodded. "One thing. Seems the bank's board of directors are having a meeting and the bank president wants to take them on a tour of their major loan projects afterward. Mr. Armstrong plans to bring them by the job site sometime this afternoon."

"I'd better check the construction schedule and see what will be going on," he said, pushing out of his chair and heading back to the outer office. "We want to look our best."

He stopped at a table against the wall and flipped the pages of a large book that served as the company's daily log, where every transaction associated with the project was entered.

Matt frowned at today's entry. "Ali's using a new painting subcontractor? Why? What was wrong with our usual team?"

Hattie ducked her head and began busily shuffling papers. "ABC Painting is a newly formed company anxious to build a reputation. Their bid was a lot lower than the contractor you usually use and they could get started sooner, too."

Something in her voice sounded suspiciously defensive, as if she were trying to hide something from him.

Matt shrugged off the feeling. He was probably imagining things. After all, he'd seen the houses for himself, and the wood staining, painting and papering looked like first-class jobs. Besides, he'd meet these people this afternoon.

Right now, he was eager to see Ali, and the banker's visit was the perfect excuse. "I'd better let Ali know about the bank's plans."

He found her seated at her desk, the phone cradled to her ear, gazing out her window. She wore a tailored pantsuit in bright pink and her hair was loose around her shoulders. He stopped in the doorway and stared, taking in the way her hair gleamed in the light, remembering how soft it had felt, how delicious it smelled. The memory tugged at him and he fought an urge to circle around her chair, lift the heavy mass of curls and nuzzle the nape of her neck.

"That sounds great. Thanks. Goodbye." Ali hung up the phone and turned, her lips curving into a wide smile when she saw him. A bevy of butterflies took wing in Matt's stomach.

"Hi! Welcome back."

"Thanks." Matt crossed the room and lowered himself into an armchair across from her desk. "Looks like you've been busy in my absence."

"You've seen the houses? What do you think?" Ali leaned forward, her eyes bright and anxious.

"Personally, I think they look great."

"And professionally?"

Matt shifted on the chair. "I'm still concerned that the interiors are too individualistic for public tastes," he admitted.

ROBIN WELLS   159

"The public doesn't buy homes, individuals do," Ali replied confidently. "You'll see I'm right when buyers start flocking to your door."

"I can't wait." Matt caught her eye and she returned his grin, her mouth flowering into a soft smile that hinted at all the unspoken things between them. Matt found himself longing to run his fingers along her cheek, to touch the gentle mounds her smile created on her cheekbones, to feel the velvety softness of her skin.

The gaze stretched into something more. Matt's heart thudded wildly as they sat, motionless, just looking at each other, sparks of attraction flying between them so thick and fast it was a miracle the smoke detector didn't detonate. Matt opened his mouth to speak, but no words came out. When he finally found his voice, it was low and husky. "Would you like to have lunch with me today?"

Ali lowered her gaze to her desk. "Oh—I, uh, can't. I'm planning to spend most of the day at the job site and I have a million things to do."

"Surely eating lunch is one of them," Matt cajoled.

"I'll grab something on the run," she said, keeping her eyes averted. "Thanks, but no."

She was saying no to more than lunch. Disappointment tightened his chest.

"Maybe some other time," he said with an indifference he didn't feel. He hoisted himself out of the chair. "I stopped by to tell you that the banker is bringing the board of directors by the job site this afternoon."

"Is anything wrong?"

"No. It's just a show-and-tell visit for some out-of-town board members, but it's important that everything looks professional. I'll be going to the bank for financing on future projects and I need to maintain their confidence and goodwill."

"I'll make sure things go smoothly."

Matt nodded as he headed for the door. He paused, a hand on the doorjamb. "Good. I'll see you out there."

Back in his office, Matt closed the door and rubbed his forehead, trying to make some sense of this maddening relationship. As far as he could determine, there were two facts. Fact One: regardless of what she pretended, Ali had no more put their attraction behind her than he had. It lay between them, unmentioned but far from forgotten, as combustible and dangerous as a stick of dynamite. Fact Two: she was determined to keep him at arm's length, to make sure that none of the sparks flying back and forth between them caused another explosion.

Well, fine, he told himself, stalking to the window. The last thing he needed was a relationship with Little Miss Mishap anyway.

Besides, Fact One and Fact Two kept him from having to deal with Fact Three: that he wanted Ali McAlester more than he'd ever wanted anything in his life; that he cared about her, craved her, and if the truth be known, was downright obsessed with her.

Loosening his tie, Matt propped his hands on either side of the glass and gazed out, not really seeing the scene before him. Instead, he saw Ali, naked and wet and glistening in candlelight. He muttered an oath and pushed off the window, aroused and distressed and as irritable as a bear with a thorn in its paw.

How ironic, how infuriating, how utterly, gut-wrenchingly *frustrating* that Ali would choose to be sensible on the one issue where he was willing to throw logic to the wind!

"Up a little bit more." Ali stood back and eyed the wainscoting two denim-clad workmen held against the entryway wall. "There—that's perfect!" She nodded in satisfaction, and one of the workmen deftly marked the spot in chalk.

"Does the wallpaper go above or below the molding?" he asked, repocketing the chalk in his shirt.

"Paint above, paper below," Ali replied. The man nodded and Ali strolled into the living room. She stopped in the middle of the room, surveying the painted walls.

"Wonderful," she breathed. The room was her favorite color, the same peachy terracotta she'd used in her own home, rag-painted over a rich tan to create an expensive, textured look. Here the warm color was accented with creamy wood-

ROBIN WELLS 161

work and an antique marble fireplace mantel Ali had found at an auction.

"You like the paint job?" asked a masculine voice behind her.

Ali spun around to find Derrick Atchison standing in the doorway. She stretched out a hand and smiled. "I love it!"

"Thanks." He beamed as he shook her hand, then looked down, scuffing his boot on the cement floor. "I really appreciate your giving me the work, Ali. They told me in the alcohol rehab center that it wouldn't be easy to turn over a new leaf." He pulled off his painter's cap and self-consciously rubbed his ear. "I've got a pretty lousy track record in this town, and it's going to take a while to earn people's trust. Thanks for giving me a chance."

"It takes a lot of courage to admit to a problem like alcoholism—and even more courage to overcome it," Ali said softly.

Derrick swallowed. "Yeah, well, it takes just as much courage for people like you and Matt and Hank to have faith in me. I still can't believe Hank loaned me the money to start my own business." He shook his head wonderingly. "I just want you to know I won't let you down. I'm determined to stay clean and sober, and I really appreciate you and Matt giving me a second chance."

No point in telling him Matt didn't have a clue. She patted his arm. "You've done a great job, and I'll be happy to tell anyone who asks. Feel free to use me as a reference."

"Thanks, Ali." He reached out and gave her a quick hug, his voice suspiciously gruff. "I'd better go give my guys a hand."

Ali watched him amble toward the kitchen, wondering what Matt's reaction would be.

Just thinking of Matt made a little shiver run down her arms. Ali rubbed her arms and crossed the room, heading for the staircase to check the progress of the upstairs bedrooms.

During the two weeks that Matt had been gone, she'd entertained a lot of fantasies about him. The most outlandish centered around the idea that a relationship might actually be possible. If they were both willing to make a few concessions, if they both made up their minds to appreciate the differences between them, if Matt would just *bend* a little, maybe, just *maybe* things could work out.

Ali's fingers trailed absently along the banister as she climbed the stairs. She'd nearly agreed to lunch today. No, that wasn't right; she'd nearly agreed to much more.

Ali drifted into the master bedroom. Mercy, it was tempting. In so many ways, Matt was everything she'd ever dreamed of in a man.

Physically, for example. Just being in the same room with him made her skin feel sensitized and tingly and hungry for his touch. And when she thought about the way he kissed her—the gentle, urgent insistence of his lips, the clean male scent of his skin, the hard, muscular planes of his body pressed against her—she grew breathless and restless and aroused all over again.

But the part of Matt that had completely, irretrievably stolen her heart had nothing to do with the physical. Underneath that tough exterior he was kind, decent and generous, and he'd proven it in dozens of ways—by quietly handling the details after Robert's death, by helping paint her house, by being so warm and understanding when she'd talked about her mother....

The problem was that he was also rigid and controlling and stubborn. She wanted—*needed*—a man who viewed her as an equal partner. She refused to have a life like her mother's, to be married to a man who pulled her strings like a marionette's.

Which brought up a whole other issue. Matt had made it clear he didn't want to ever get married again, and Ali wanted the works. Love. Commitment. Children.

She wrapped her arms tightly across her chest, rubbing her hands along her sweater. She'd been right to tell him no, she told herself.

So why was she standing here feeling as empty as the unfurnished room, ready to burst into tears in the middle of the day?

She had to stop dwelling on Matt. Turning abruptly, she clattered down the hardwood stairs and out the door.

The wind whipped her hair and cooled her cheeks, helping to clear her mind. She scurried to the next house, the one she called the gingerbread cottage, forcing her thoughts back to her work. She was decorating this house in crisp ginghams and fresh country prints, and she was anxious to see what progress had been made on it.

Halfway across the lawn, she felt a sudden, sharp burning in her eye. She stopped and blinked hard as tears coursed down her cheeks. "Darned contact lenses," she muttered. The wind had blown something into her eye and the tiny speck was trapped behind the lens. She would have to remove her contact.

She tugged at the corner of her eye and popped out the lens, only to have a strong gust of wind blow it away.

"Oh, no!" she moaned, dropping to her knees and frantically searching among the leaves.

"Did you lose something, Miss McAlester?"

Ali looked up to see Big Jim Bentmore looming over her, his ruddy face blurred by her lopsided vision.

"A contact lens. It's part of my only pair, and I'm blind without them. I dropped it right in here somewhere."

"We'll find it for you." He turned toward the house, cupped his hands and shouted. "Hey, guys—we need help over here!"

Before she knew what was happening, eight workers had gathered around her. "We need to find Miss McAlester's contact lens," Jim explained.

"What do we look for?" asked a large, burly man.

"Something small and shiny," Ali said. "Our best bet is to try to see the light reflecting off it. It helps to get your face down low and look at the ground at an angle."

All eight men hit the ground and began crawling cautiously through the leaves, their heads cocked to the side, their backsides in the air.

"The next house is just over this hill, gentlemen." Matt led the way to the gingerbread cottage, pleased with the way the visit was going. The bankers had raved about the first house, and it was the simplest one of all. If they liked that one, they were sure to love the next two.

As he topped the crest, he froze in his tracks and blinked hard. *What the hell was going on?*

He stared in disbelief at the sight before him. His work crew was crawling in the dirt like a bunch of anteaters, their heads down, their rumps aimed at the sky. One trim, shapely back-side clad in bright pink stood out from the rest.

He'd recognize that rump anywhere, he thought grimly. *Ali.*

Matt felt his temper build like a thundercloud. He'd told her the bankers were coming; how dare she stage a scene like this?

Time enough to deal with her later. Right now he needed to try to salvage the situation. Maybe he could steer the bankers in the other direction.

Too late. The five men in business suits had joined him on the hill and were staring down at the scene below.

"I found it!" roared Big Jim, jumping in the air with an upraised arm, his enormous belly jiggling. The work crew noisily applauded and whistled as Jim handed something to Ali.

"What in heaven's name is going on here?" Mr. Armstrong demanded, his round face puckered in alarm.

Ali whirled toward them. "Matt! Mr. Armstrong!" She scrambled up the hill, extended her hand to the banker and fixed him with an enchanting smile. "So nice to see you! Sorry we looked so undignified just now, but I dropped a contact lens and the men were helping me find it."

"I see." Placated, the broad man patted her hand and smiled. "Glad you found it, dear. Gentlemen, this is the little lady responsible for the interiors of these homes. Ali, I'd like to introduce you to the bank's board of directors."

She had charmed her way right out of the situation. The sense of relief Matt knew he should be feeling was overshadowed by a sense of outrage. He hated being so out of control. He'd told her the bankers were coming this afternoon, dammit, and he'd specifically requested that she make sure things were in order. How dare she completely ignore his instructions?

"Matt, why don't you take these gentlemen on a tour of the cottage? I'll see to my contact, then I'll be right back to join you."

Matt had no choice but to comply as Ali scurried off to fix her contact lens. She caught up with the group on the porch of the house with the turret.

Mr. Armstrong turned to her and beamed. "Ali, I love what you've done to the interiors."

Ali smiled. "Thank you. You'll have to come back for the open house and see them with furnishings. Did Matt tell you about it?"

"No," said Mr. Armstrong, casting a glance at Matt that indicated he considered it a serious oversight. "But I saw the ad in the Sunday newspaper. My wife can't wait to come."

Ad in the newspaper? Why wasn't he consulted about this?

"I'm delighted to hear that."

They stepped onto the porch and Ali opened the door. Matt hung back until the rest of the group had entered the house. He brushed by Ali, his shoulder touching hers in the doorway. Despite his anger, a shiver of attraction shot down his arm. The fact only increased his irritation; she was making him as out of control as she was, and he didn't like it one little bit.

"Sorry," she whispered, stepping back.

"You damn well should be," he muttered stiffly. The air was charged between them. Their eyes collided, and Matt read the confusion in her wide gray gaze as it clashed against his own.

The woman had no idea she'd done anything wrong, didn't even have a clue why he was upset. The realization rankled all the more, because it made *him* feel like *he* was being unreasonable.

Which he most certainly was not. Matt blew out an exasperated blast of air as Ali darted from the doorway. He ran a finger around the neck of his shirt, which suddenly seemed to have grown too tight and too hot, and followed the others into the living room, where murmurs of approval were coming from the board members.

Ali addressed the group with ease and graciousness, giving them the history of the fireplace mantel, then directing them into the kitchen. Despite his irritation, he admired her aplomb. She was good—damned good. She had them in the palm of her hand. For some reason, the thought aggravated him all the more.

He tagged along as the group made the turn into the dining room where three painters were at work, their backs to the crowd. The man standing on the stepladder looked vaguely familiar. Matt stared at the back of his head as Ali talked, trying to place him. When he turned to dip his brush in the paint can, recognition poured over Matt like a pitcher of cold water.

"Derrick! What the hell are *you* doing here?"

"His new company is handling the painting and papering," Ali offered quickly. "Their bid was more reasonable than the one from our regular subcontractor and they could get started sooner. Since you told me to go ahead and handle the interiors, I hired them while you were out of town. I think they've done an excellent job, don't you?"

Matt stifled a sharp retort as the board members nodded their concurrence. There was nothing to be gained from making a scene, no matter how badly he itched to give her a piece of his mind.

How dare she hire Derrick, knowing full well how much he disliked the man? And why hadn't he been informed? He felt like a fool, not knowing what was going on in his own company.

The whole situation made his blood boil. Matt seethed in silence as Ali continued to play gracious hostess.

"Everything looks great here, Matt," Mr. Armstrong said as the group returned to their cars. "We're pleased and proud that Frontier Fidelity could play a role in your project."

"Yes, indeed. This is just the sort of creative thinking we're looking for," chimed in the board president. "Let us know whenever you have a project that needs financing and we'll give you priority treatment."

He should be thrilled, but he was too angry to appreciate the good news.

"Thank you, sir," he managed, trying to muster an appropriate tone of gratitude. He curled and uncurled his fingers, biding his time, waiting until the cars drove out of sight before he turned to Ali.

She gave him a smile bright enough to charm a snake. "The visit went well, don't you think?"

"Do you really want to know what I think?" Matt snapped.

Ali's gray eyes grew wary. She drew herself to her full height and squared her shoulders. "I have a feeling I don't, but go ahead and tell me anyway."

"I think it's a miracle they didn't call the note on the spot, the way you greeted them with the entire crew on their knees like a bunch of praying mantises."

"They were helping me find my contact lens, for Pete's sake!" Ali threw her palms up in a gesture of exasperation. "Things don't always go as planned, Matt, but that doesn't mean they're going wrong."

Matt loomed over her. "It does when I don't even know what's going on in my own company."

"What are you talking about?"

"I'll tell you what I'm talking about," he growled. "Why didn't I know ads were running in Sunday's paper?"

"I would have discussed it with you, but you were out of town."

"That's no excuse." He glowered at her. "I didn't authorize any advertising expenditures and I didn't approve any ad copy."

"It was a very inexpensive, simple ad—"

"That's not the point! I'm supposed to approve all expenditures." He frowned so hard his brows nearly met, the thought of the next topic inciting him like a red flag in front of a bull. "Worst of all, Ali, why the hell did you hire Derrick Atchison? The moment my back was turned, you deliberately contracted a man you know I despise."

"If you'd just listen to reason for a moment—"

Matt threw out his hands. "Listen to reason? What reason could you possibly have for hiring a low-down, scum-sucking river rat like that?"

Ali's arms went rigid at her sides. "It must be nice to be perfect," she said icily. "It must be wonderful to be so sure that your way is the only way, to be so far above reproach that you don't dare sully yourself by associating with anyone who's ever made a mistake. People *can* change, you know." She raised an eyebrow meaningfully. "Or perhaps you don't. It's a concept you should investigate, Matt."

"Just what in blue blazes do you mean by that?"

She stared him down. "I mean it would do you good to learn a little tolerance and flexibility. You don't always have to be in control, you know. Other people can occasionally manage without your guidance."

"If you're talking about yourself, and I assume you are, the only thing you seem able to manage is leaving havoc in your wake and escaping total disaster by the skin of your teeth."

Her gaze was hot enough to leave a sunburn. "You'll only have to put up with it for two more weeks. When the open house is over, I'll be out of your life forever."

"Won't be a moment too soon," Matt retorted. "In fact, why don't we put it in writing? I'll have my attorney send you the papers finalizing the buy-out agreement."

"Sounds good to me. I have no interest in working with a know-it-all, stuffed-shirt control freak." She tilted her chin up. "As soon as this project is over, I'm moving back to Dallas. With any luck, I'll never set eyes on you again." She whipped around and marched off, leaving Matt to glare after her.

Well, fine. That was what he'd wanted all along.

Wasn't it?

So why did the sight of her retreating back make his heart plummet like a dropped roofing hammer?

Chapter Thirteen

Matt flipped to the last page of the thick legal document that had come in the afternoon mail, his gaze scanning the page until it lit on Ali's signature, written in a bold, angry scrawl.

She'd signed the buy-out agreement. Effective midnight Saturday, he'd be the sole owner of Cimarron Homebuilders. By all rights, he should feel elated. But for some reason the victory left him flat and empty.

"What's with you and Ali?" Hattie asked, handing him the rest of his mail.

"You mean this?" He pointed to the contract. "I planned to buy out her shares all along."

"I was referring to the fact you haven't spoken two words to each other all week long."

Less than that, Matt thought grimly. He'd gone out of his way to steer clear of her ever since their argument. He'd driven past the job site without stopping on four different occasions because he'd seen her car there, and at the office, he'd taken to confining himself behind closed doors.

But he wasn't the only one going out of his way to avoid contact. When he'd accidentally encountered her in the office hallway she'd treated him like he had terminal halitosis and it might be contagious.

Matt leaned back in his chair and looked up at his secretary. "You might say we had a difference of opinion."

Hattie eyed him reprovingly. "Well, you need to straighten it out. You're grumpy as a plucked buzzard. Besides, you'll have to be civil to each other at the open house on Saturday and it'll be a whole lot easier if you iron things out before then."

Matt waved the document. "There's nothing to iron out. As soon as Ali's little shindig is over, so is our partnership."

Hattie shook her head. "If you let that girl go, it'll be the worst mistake of your life."

"The worst mistake of my life was having anything to do with her in the first place."

The older woman frowned. "I don't understand you, Matt. Ali's doing you a big favor, but you're acting like she's an enemy. The photographer for that national magazine will be in town tomorrow to shoot the houses for a layout, the newspaper is doing a feature about them and half the town is coming to the open house. Your firm is going to be famous and those houses are going to sell like hotcakes. You should be thanking her instead of trying to get rid of her."

Matt scowled. "She'll probably make us look like a bunch of damn fools. No telling what she and her open house committee are doing to those houses." He drummed his fingers on the tabletop. "What's she up to today?"

"Arranging furniture. It was all delivered this morning."

Matt pushed back his chair. "I'd better go see."

Hattie wagged her finger at him. "You mark my word, Matt. You'll miss that gal when she's gone." She marched out of his office in a rustle of starched cotton.

Matt rose and pulled on his jacket. Hattie knew nothing about it, he thought stubbornly.

He missed her already.

He let out a long sigh. He must be deranged; he seemed to be obsessed with her. The fact she was complete anathema to him did nothing to keep her from taunting his thoughts all day and all night, regardless of what he was doing or where he was—in his car, at his desk, in his bed . . .

Especially in bed. Sleep had become an elusive stranger that dodged him all night as he chased after thoughts of Ali.

Dadblast it all! She was driving him insane, and it just proved how right he was to want nothing further to do with the woman. Once she cleared out of Hillsboro, maybe life would return to normal. Maybe he'd finally be able to eat and sleep and focus his thoughts again. Maybe he'd even be able to stop feeling like a refugee at his own place of business.

He raked a hand through his hair, shoved the legal document in his coat pocket and strode out the door.

Her car was nowhere in sight when he pulled up in front of the turreted house twenty minutes later. Instead of relief, however, he felt a perverse sense of disappointment. It was a good thing this blasted open house was nearly over with, he thought darkly. Her absence had begun to bother him just as much as her presence. He couldn't wait until she went back to Dallas and quit tormenting him.

The sky was threatening and the air smelled like rain as Matt strode to the door. He closed the heavy beveled glass door behind him, shutting out the loud rustle of the wind in the trees, and flipped on a light against the premature darkness of the impending storm.

When he turned around, the sight that greeted him stopped him in his tracks.

"Jiminy Christmas!" What the heck had Ali done to the place?

He ran a hand through his hair and looked around, his astonished gaze taking in the polished mahogany furniture, the striking paintings, the Oriental rugs, the candlesticks, lamps, and dozens of other small touches that made the room warm and alive. It even smelled good, like cinnamon and berries.

He didn't know what he'd expected. Maybe a few sticks of furniture here and there, a couple of goofy pictures on the wall, some artsy-schmartsy touches. He sure hadn't expected the house to look like a warm, inviting, elegant home. If he didn't know better, he'd think the owners had run out on an errand and would be back at any minute.

Matt strolled through the house, taking in the collection of porcelain pigs in the kitchen, the child's wagon used as an end table in the playroom, the surprising, tasteful mix of antiques and new pieces in room after room.

It was beautiful, all right, with just a touch of whimsy and humor. Just like Ali.

Matt gave a low whistle as he finished his tour. The place was nothing short of spectacular—a dream home, a regular showplace.

Which was, after all, what she'd set out to do.

The realization stopped him short, sharpening the dull ache he always felt when he thought about Ali into a wrenching pain. He sat on the stairs, his head in his hands, his heart at his feet.

He'd been a fool. An utter, stubborn fool. He'd completely misjudged her. His preconceptions had blinded him, preventing him from seeing what a bright, capable, creative woman she was.

Worse, he'd been a jerk. A first-class, stuffed-shirt, closed-minded jerk. He'd treated her like a child in need of supervision instead of an equal partner. He'd vastly underestimated her skills.

Vastly underestimated *her*. He swore under his breath, all of his anger at her fizzling like old soda pop.

Hell, she couldn't help the fact that she'd lost a contact lens. And he *had* told her to handle the interiors, which gave her the right to hire anyone she pleased. And so what if she'd run an ad in the paper without discussing it with him? He'd been out of town. As half owner of the company, she'd had every right.

Why had he made such a big deal out of it? Was he looking for reasons to find fault with her?

Matt loosened his tie, his heart sagging under the weight of the answer.

Yes. He'd been looking for something to discredit her, for anything to stem the growing tide of tenderness that welled up inside him whenever he saw her, whenever he thought of her. His anger had been nothing but a cardboard firewall, a flimsy attempt to protect himself from the torch he was carrying for her.

Now that he'd realized it, what the heck was he going to do about it?

He heard a noise on the first floor and jumped to his feet. Maybe it was Ali. Feeling more alive than he had in days, he raced down the stairs and headed toward the sound. He rounded the corner, his heart pounding, and nearly bumped into Derrick Atchison.

Matt scowled in disappointment and dislike. "I thought you were finished. What are you doing here?"

"Ali told me the movers scuffed the doorway when they brought in the furniture today, so I came back to touch it up." He straightened and stood, wiping his hands on his white painter's pants. "I haven't had a chance to thank you for giving me a chance on this job, Matt. It was mighty big of you— especially after everything that's happened between us. My counselor at the alcohol treatment center told me I'm lucky to have friends like you and Ali. Not everyone gets a chance to start over so early in recovery, and I want you to know I'm grateful." He stuck out his hand.

Derrick was an alcoholic? Matt stared at his outstretched hand as the words sank in. A problem like that would explain his inability to keep a job, his erratic life-style, his lack of responsibility, his crude behavior.

And now he was trying to recover?

Of course. That was why Ali had given him the painting contract—she was trying to help him get back on his feet.

Matt inwardly winced. She'd tried to explain, but he wouldn't listen. He'd ranted and raved and railed at her when her motivations had been kind and good-hearted and generous.

Matt shifted uneasily, feeling about two inches high. He had to find her. He didn't know what he was going to say or do, but he somehow had to set things right. He only hoped he wasn't too late.

He grasped Derrick's hand and gave it a firm shake. "I'm glad you're straightening out your life. Looks like you have a bright future ahead, judging from the job you did here."

Derrick grinned broadly and pumped Matt's hand. "Thanks."

"Do you know where Ali is?"

"Last time I saw her, she was headed home."

Matt started for the door. "Lock up when you leave—looks like a bad storm is coming."

Derrick nodded. "Sure thing. I'm almost done."

Matt strode purposefully back to his truck. The wind whipped the trees and scuttled the clouds across the sky as he yanked open the door of the pickup and climbed inside. It was just like Ali to give someone another chance, he thought as he started the engine. One question reverberated in his mind as he guided the truck away from the curb.

Would she give him another chance, too?

Black clouds boiled in the eastern sky as Matt drove to Ali's house. This time of year in Oklahoma, clouds like that could be dangerous. Matt flipped on the truck radio and scanned the channels for a weather report.

"A tornado warning is in effect until nine o'clock this evening," an announcer intoned. "Funnels have been sighted ten miles east of Hillsboro, moving in a westerly direction. Residents should be prepared to take shelter."

Matt stepped on the gas, intent on reaching Ali. If anything happened to her . . .

The thought made his blood run cold. The first drops of rain splattered on his windshield as another thought struck him, this one with the force of a cyclone.

I love her.

Stunned, Matt stared at the road. Water beaded and ran on the glass, blurring his vision, and he absently switched on the wipers. Until this moment, he'd had no idea what he was going to do or say when he saw her. He'd been acting purely on impulse, an unheard of state of affairs for him. And now he knew why.

He loved her. Why hadn't he realized it before now?

The swishing rubber blades seemed to clear his mind as well as the windshield. The truth stretched in front of him like the white lines on the road, stark and bright and laid out in a row.

All of his efforts to avoid her, to find fault with her, to be angry at her, were nothing more than feeble attempts to deny an undeniable truth.

He loved her. He rubbed his forehead, trying to puzzle out how such a thing could have happened without his knowledge, without his permission. He hadn't planned to fall in love with anyone, much less with Ali. He had no intention of repeating the mistake he'd made with Elise.

The rain began to fall in earnest, thundering on the roof of the truck as Matt was struck with another jarring thought. Maybe the mistake he'd made with Elise wasn't falling in love, wasn't even getting married. Maybe the mistake was just picking the wrong woman.

The wipers sluiced back and forth, the glass growing cleaner and clearer. Ali was completely different from Elise, from any woman Matt had ever known. It stood to reason that a relationship with her would be different, too. She was warm and kind and giving, the type of woman who loved animals and children, who knew how to make a house a home, who brightened a room just by walking into it.

Who'd brightened his *life* just by walking into it.

Matt squinted, as much in concentration as in an effort to see through the driving rain. Yes, she was unpredictable, and yes, confusion *did* seem to surround her like a cloud of perfume, but so did love and joy and a zest for life.

Matt's fingers tightened on the steering wheel. His life was sorely lacking in all those things. It might be well-ordered and predictable, but it was also sterile and cold and empty.

What was it Ali had said? *Things don't always go according to plan, but that doesn't mean they're going wrong.*

He pressed his foot to the accelerator, anxious to close the distance separating them. If he was ever going to have a chance at happiness, real happiness, this was it. One thing was for sure: life with Ali would never be boring.

The wail of a siren keened through the air and Matt rolled down his window to better hear it, ignoring the rain splattering his face. It wasn't an approaching ambulance or a police car as he'd first thought; it was the town's emergency warning system cautioning people to take shelter.

Alarm raced through him. He turned up the volume of the radio but got only static. The local station was off the air.

He peered up at the blackened sky, which seemed to be getting darker as he neared Ali's home, and was gripped by a cold fear. He'd seen some bad storms in his thirty-one years, but he'd never seen anything like this.

His mouth set in a grim line, he drove as fast as he dared, his hands gripping the steering wheel so tightly his knuckles ached.

He said a silent prayer as he turned into Ali's subdivision, then felt his heart plummet to the floorboard as he saw the first house, roofless and battered. It was the Johnson place, one of the first homes he and Robert had built. Thank goodness the Johnsons had been transferred to Chicago and the house was vacant. Matt realized he should feel something at seeing his handiwork in such a state, should have some sense of loss, but all of his emotions were focused on the terrifying fact that a tornado had indeed passed this way.

Ali's home was around the next curve. He gunned the engine, his mouth dry, his pulse pounding in his throat. He tried to tell himself that tornadoes were fickle, that they could hit a house and leave the one next to it standing, but what he saw confirmed his worst fears.

"Oh, God, no," he whispered.

The house was leveled, a mangled mess of boards and shingles and pipes and wire. Three walls of one interior room were all that remained upright. The rest of the building was a chaotic heap, as if a giant hand had picked it up, crushed it like a potato chip and tossed it into the air.

Matt jerked the truck into Park and jumped out before it had even stopped rolling.

"Ali!" he called. Despair weighted his chest. She could be lying injured or—God forbid!—dead under any of the piles of rubbish. Where should he even begin?

He stood in the downpour, wet to the skin, straining to see a clue or hear a sign, silently willing her to somehow beckon him.

"Ali!"

Was that a whimper he heard, or just the rain echoing off the wreckage? His head jerked in the direction he thought it came from and called again. "Ali! Where are you, honey?"

There it was again! It sounded like it was coming from the center of the ruins, near the area where the three walls still stood. A spark of hope lit Matt's heart and propelled him into the wreckage.

His peripheral vision caught sight of something dangling above him. He glanced up to see wires trailing from a power line.

Careful—the electric lines are down. The thought brought an impatient curse. He was forced to slow his steps, to cautiously pick his way through the rubble as if it were a mine field.

"Ali, honey, I'm coming. Tell me where you are," he called.

An eerie wail drifted back to him, causing his adrenaline to surge. Matt sent a another silent petition to God and forged ahead, dreading what he might find, fearing he might get there too late.

He finally stepped over a large section of roof and into what had been her bathroom. He stared at the counter, where a wicker basket of potpourri, a perfume bottle and a crystal soap dish bizarrely stood in perfect order, the only testimony to the maelstrom they'd endured the tiny shards of broken mirror that covered them like prisms from a chandelier.

Turning, Matt saw the enormous tub—and inside it, a very wet, very frightened, black and white dog.

Flipper let out a mournful whine and tried to scramble up the slick marble.

"It was you making the noise," Matt muttered, bending to scoop up the animal with one hand. He tucked the shivering little dog inside his shirt and fought a sickening wave of disappointment. "Where is she, boy?"

The little dog wriggled and tried to lick his face. Matt pushed him lower in his shirt. "If ever you needed to know a trick, this is it, boy," Matt told the mutt grimly. He waded back to his truck, tossed the little dog on the seat and slammed the door.

Turning, Matt cupped his hands around his mouth. "Ali!" he bellowed. Only the wind and the rain responded.

Where the hell was she? If she'd run for cover, surely she would have taken the dog with her. He should have found them together.

Maybe, just maybe, she wasn't here after all. A glimmer of hope resuscitated in Matt's soul.

Her car. I'll look for her car. Ali always parked in the garage.

Matt maneuvered toward the heap that had once been her garage and dug like crazy, channeling his anxiety into raw physical energy until he'd cleared away enough rubble to know that her car was not there.

Not here. She's not here. Matt felt a tremendous lightening, an enormous sense of relief—then his heart plunged again with his very next thought.

Then where the hell was she? He stood in the pelting rain, his mouth creased into a grim frown.

The Victorian Village. If Ali had known the storm was coming, he was certain she'd go there to keep an eye on the borrowed furnishings.

He bounded toward the truck, flung open the door and was greeted by a frantic Flipper, who did a back flip on the seat. "Hang on, fella," Matt muttered as he screeched around the corner. "You're in for a ride."

Ali perched on the living room window seat inside the turreted house and stared out at the driving rain, watching it bend the branches of a tall oak. The downpour seemed to be letting up a little. Thank heavens the worst of the storm had bypassed the Victorian Village.

She hoped it had bypassed everyone she cared about, as well—Susan, Hank, Hattie, Matt . . .

Matt. The thought of him stirred a familiar pang in her chest. She tried to block him from her thoughts, to steer her mind away from him, but his memory was as stubborn as the man himself, drawing her like a sore tooth draws the tongue.

She'd been miserable ever since their argument, unable to eat or sleep or find pleasure in anything. Even completing the interiors of the homes had brought her little satisfaction.

Just three more days and her goal would be accomplished. Just three more days and she'd move back to Dallas to start her own interior design firm. Just three more days and she'd never see Matt again.

She gave a deep sigh and rose to her feet. She should feel relief or anticipation or something—something, anything but this vast, aching emptiness.

She paced the room, inventorying all the reasons she'd been right to end to their relationship. He was bossy, he was intolerant, he didn't trust her judgment and he'd made it clear he never intended to marry again.

So what if he was also kind and thoughtful and funny and smart and sexy as all get-out? He was the wrong man for her. She knew that on an intellectual level.

Why couldn't her foolish heart get the message?

A noise in the back of the house made her start. One of the workmen must have returned, she thought, hurrying toward the sound, wondering who it was and what would have brought him out in this downpour.

She stopped abruptly as she rounded the kitchen doorway and clutched a hand to her chest. "Matt!"

He was dripping wet, so wet a puddle pooled at his feet. A rivulet of water ran from his hair down the back of his neck.

"Thank God, you're all right, Ali." His voice was rough and urgent, his eyes dark and intense. He crossed the room and clasped her in a bear hug, drenching her, damply imprinting himself on her T-shirt and jeans. He smelled like rain and wet denim. She was too shocked to protest; instead, she swayed against him, soaking up the feel of his long, hard length pressed against her, of his warm skin radiating through his soggy clothes, of his heart thrumming next to her own.

The void in her chest filled with warmth as her heart opened and blossomed. Dear Lord, how she'd missed him! Not seeing him, not talking to him, had been like not being alive.

The thought raised a mental red flag. She'd avoided him for a reason, she reminded herself. A good reason—her own self-preservation. She'd do well to remember that fact.

She stiffened and pulled back, straightening her damp shirt. "What were you doing out in the storm?"

"Looking for you."

Did he think she was so addlebrained she needed a keeper? She lifted her chin. "This may come as a surprise to you, Matt, but I happen to have the sense to come in out of the rain." Her gaze swept him from head to toe. "Unlike someone I could mention."

He ran a hand through his hair, spraying out drops of water, and regarded her somberly. "Ali, I'm afraid I have some bad news."

His quiet, grim tone alarmed her. "What is it?"

"The storm did a lot of damage to your house, honey."

She stared at him, trying to understand.

"I've got Flipper in my truck," he continued. "He's fine. But, Ali, honey—everything else is a mess."

"How bad?"

He took her hands. "Bad," he said softly. "It's leveled, honey. Everything's gone."

Her head swam. *I must be in shock,* she thought. Because the only part of all he'd just said that had any meaning at all to her was a single word, a word that had no relation to the news he'd just broken to her.

Honey. He called me honey.

It was what he'd called her when he'd kissed her, when he'd sent her senses spinning and her heart singing, and hearing it now nearly undid what little composure she had left.

Ali shook her head, trying to clear it, and seized upon another incongruous fact.

"You went to my house and got Flipper?"

Matt nodded.

Don't read anything into it, she told herself sternly. She couldn't afford to let the hope budding inside her take root and grow.

His hands slid up her shoulders. "Ali, when I saw your house, I went crazy. If anything had happened to you..."

Why, oh, *why* did he have to trot out his kind, caring side? It was killing her, seeing this part of him that she loved, knowing he felt nothing but a sense of responsibility toward her because she was his late partner's sister.

She turned away and tried to hide her aching heart under a show of bravado. "It's a shame about the house, but it could be worse, Matt. It's fully insured. Besides, I'm moving back to Dallas."

Matt grasped her arms and turned her back toward him. "Ali, I don't want you to go."

Her heart caught in her throat. She stared at him, not daring to breathe, not daring to think.

"I came by earlier and saw what you'd done with the interiors. They look great. Better than great. In fact, they look so good they made me realize what a fool I've been."

He reached into his pocket and pulled out a document she recognized as the buy-out agreement she'd signed yesterday. As she watched in astonishment, he ripped it in two.

He'd just destroyed the papers that gave him sole ownership of the firm—the one thing he'd wanted more than anything in the world! She stared in amazement as he tossed the torn pages on the floor and stepped toward her, again taking her hands.

It vaguely registered in her mind that it was completely unlike Matt to ever throw anything on the floor. She gazed up at him in bewilderment.

"I want you to stay on as my partner," he said softly. "You did a hell of a job on the interiors—not just on the design, but on budgeting the project, managing the subcontractors and overseeing the work. You're a real asset to the company."

Ali gaped at him, trying to absorb his meaning, her pulse pounding. If he wanted her as his partner, it meant he had confidence in her. If he had confidence in her, it meant he valued her opinion, felt she had something to contribute, wanted her input.

It meant he trusted her. Her heart fluttered and unfolded like the wings of a bird.

"Your brother would have been so pleased and proud." His voice was low and husky. "I know I am."

Ali stood stock-still, letting the words pour over her, feeling their sweetness, still afraid to take them to heart. She couldn't have spoken a word even if she could have thought of anything to say.

His eyes glittered in the storm-darkened dusk as he stepped toward her. Her heart hammered in her chest.

"I owe you an apology," he continued. "I've been unreasonable and out of line and stubborn. I hope you can forgive me."

Ali wasn't sure if the drumming in her ears was caused by the rain on the roof or her own pounding heart. He took a step toward her and placed his hands on her arms, making her pulse skip and skitter.

"You were right about everything, Ali. Including the fact I need to change."

Her heart soared as high and fast as a guided missile. Her voice came out breathless, as if there weren't enough oxygen in the air. "What sort of changes are you thinking of making?"

"For starters, I'm through trying to control everything." His fingers slid up her arms. "This storm made me face some hard truths, and one of them is, I can't control anything or anyone but myself." He pulled her closer, his gaze direct and earnest. "I used to think I could avoid disappointment by planning everything out and avoiding surprises. But life is about surprises, and not all of them are bad. So I've decided to try to follow your advice. From here on out, I'm going to try to loosen up and enjoy life as it comes."

His eyes were the color of old whiskey, and the look he gave her was just as intoxicating. "There's another change I'd like to make." He hesitated, his fingers tightening on her upper arms. "I'd like to change my marital status. That is, if you'll have me."

Her heart slammed against her ribs. She gazed up at him, barely daring to breathe.

"I love you, Ali."

The words fell on her ears like music. She stared into his eyes, spellbound, as her heart danced and sang within.

"I've fallen for you hook, line and fishing lure. And I want to marry you." His voice was soft and sure. So were his hands as they moved to her back. His eyes held a warm, tender light as he gazed down at her. "Do you think you could learn to love a stubborn old cuss like me?"

Joy flooded her chest, filling the hollow spot in her heart, overflowing into her soul. "Oh, Matt. Don't you know I already do?"

She flung her arms around his neck so suddenly and with such force that he stepped back to get his balance, then slipped on the wet ceramic tile. They both toppled to the floor, landing in a soggy heap.

He pulled her on top of him and gave a soft chuckle into her hair. "You keep me off balance, Ali. You knock me off my feet, you bowl me over, you make the earth move." He wrapped his arms around her and gazed into her eyes, his lips curving into a grin that promised to become a kiss at any moment. "What more could any man want?"

"Maybe he could want this," she whispered, lowering her lips to his and smothering him with a kiss as warm and loving and wild as their lifetime together promised to be.

Epilogue

Ali opened the antique locket dangling around her neck and glanced at the watch inside. "Quitting time," she announced, crossing the room to take down the Open House sign taped to the front door. "It went well, don't you think?"

Susan pulled up the voluminous skirt of her yellow Victorian gown and plopped down on a velvet love seat. "Are you kidding? You've had hundreds of people through here—not to mention two TV crews and photographers from newspapers in Hillsboro, Tulsa and Oklahoma City. Everyone raved about the houses and thought the period costumes were pure genius."

Ali smiled and sat down beside her. "More importantly, we've gotten offers on all three houses and dozens of prospective buyers for the others."

Susan placed her hand on Ali's arm. "You've done a fantastic job, Ali. Robert would have been so pleased."

The thought warmed Ali's heart. "His designs will be famous when the August issue of *American Homelife* comes out. Matt thinks his blueprints will sell like crazy." She grinned at her friend. "Thanks for your help, Suze. And thanks for giving me a place to stay until after my wedding."

"My pleasure."

The door opened and Hattie bustled in, looking for all the world like a schoolmarm in her old-fashioned skirt and shawl. She grinned broadly at Ali. "Matt wants you to join him next door. Susan and I will lock up here."

As always, the thought of Matt made her heart pound. She'd been so busy she'd barely had a chance to see him all day. "Thanks, Hattie."

She hurried to the house with the turret and found Matt in the master bedroom, leaning against a post of the enormous mahogany bed. She stopped in the doorway, her pulse quickening at the sight of him in this frankly sensuous room—a room draped in lush fabrics in shades of rose and cream and deep green, with a thick Aubusson rug on the floor and candles everywhere. He'd been on her mind when she'd decorated it and seeing him in it made her stomach tighten.

He gave her a slow, devastating smile as his gaze traveled the length of her, gliding over her long lace dress. "You look beautiful. Like an old-fashioned Gibson Girl."

Her fingers flew self-consciously to her loosely upswept hair.

"Dressed in pink with your hair like that, you remind me of how you looked when I first kissed you at that wedding." Matt gave an amused shake of his head. "I should have known then my single days were numbered."

Ali grinned. "You'll get to kiss me at another wedding in just a few weeks."

"I can hardly wait. Maybe we should practice." He crossed the room, pulled her into his arms and kissed her until her knees felt like melted butter.

Ali gazed up at him, her arms still around his neck. "We need to decide on a location. I've always dreamed of a garden wedding, but knowing my luck, it'll rain and our guests will get drenched."

"Knowing your luck, they're just as likely to get drenched indoors by a fire sprinkler system." He gave a wry grin and ran a caressing finger across her cheek. "On some matters, honey, you've just got to follow your heart. If you want a garden wedding, that's what we'll have."

"I can't believe how you've mellowed," she said softly.

"I can't believe how I underestimated you." His gaze was filled with love and pride. "Today was terrific. We've got more buyers than houses, and it's all due to you."

The look in his eyes stole the breath from her lungs. "I don't deserve all the credit. Robert designed the houses and you built them."

"Yes, but we only created houses. You made them into homes. And you came up with an ingenious way of market- ing them." His hands slid down her lace sleeves. "We aren't the only ones that profited from it. The Suds 'n Duds sisters racked up orders right and left, and the old geezer who owns the antique store said he made more sales today than he nor- mally does in a month. Even the starving artist did well—al- though her nose ring didn't exactly go with the decor."

Ali smiled. Matt moved so close she could see the golden facets in his tawny eyes and feel his breath against her cheek. A shiver of attraction raced up her spine.

"I have a surprise for you, Ali."

"*You* have a surprise for *me?*"

He grinned and shrugged. "I wanted to show you I'm not so dreadfully predictable after all."

"What is it?"

His brown eyes danced. "This house and everything in it."

Ali stared at him for a long moment, too flabbergasted to speak. "You're kidding," she finally managed.

"I'm not. Here's the deed." He plucked a document off the bureau and handed it to her, his teeth flashing in a smile. "And I bought all the furnishings. You spent a lot of time and ef- fort arranging everything the way you wanted it, and it would be a shame to send it all back to the stores."

A jolt of joy shot through her. What a wonderful, amazing man she was marrying!

"Oh, Matt," she breathed, pulling him to her and kissing him until they were both drugged and senseless.

When they finally came up for air, Ali was a tangle of rose lace and tousled hair and misty eyes. Matt thought she'd never looked lovelier.

"Do you like your surprise?" he asked.

"It's wonderful. *You're* wonderful." She wrapped her arms around his neck and beamed up at him, pure rapture shining in her eyes.

It made his heart do somersaults to think he'd put that expression on her face. "You know, there's something to be said for this surprise business after all," he murmured, lowering his head and settling down to the task of discovering new ways to surprise her further.

* * * * * *

If you enjoyed THE WEDDING KISS, be sure to pick up Robin's next novel, HUSBAND AND WIFE....AGAIN, coming March 1997 from Silhouette Romance.

This October, be the first to read these wonderful
authors as they make their dazzling debuts!

Women to Watch

THE WEDDING KISS by Robin Wells
(Silhouette Romance #1185)
A reluctant bachelor rescues the woman he loves
from the man she's about to marry—and turns into
a willing groom himself!

THE SEX TEST by Patty Salier
(Silhouette Desire #1032)
A pretty professor learns there's more to making love
than meets the eye when she takes lessons from
a sexy stranger.

IN A FAMILY WAY by Julia Mozingo
(Special Edition #1062)
A woman without a past finds shelter in the arms of
a handsome rancher. Can she trust him to protect
her unborn child?

UNDER COVER OF THE NIGHT by Roberta Tobeck
(Intimate Moments #744)
A rugged government agent encounters the woman he has
always loved. But past secrets could threaten their future.

DATELESS IN DALLAS by Samantha Carter
(Yours Truly)
A hapless reporter investigates how to find the perfect
mate—and winds up falling for her handsome rival!

Don't miss the brightest stars of tomorrow!

Only from  *Silhouette*®

Take 4 bestselling love stories FREE

Plus get a FREE surprise gift!

Special Limited-time Offer

Mail to Silhouette Reader Service®

P.O. Box 609
Fort Erie, Ontario
L2A 5X3

YES! Please send me 4 free Silhouette Romance™ novels and my free surprise gift. Then send me 6 brand-new novels every month, which I will receive months before they appear in bookstores. Bill me at the low price of $3.00 each plus 25¢ delivery and GST*. That's the complete price and a savings of over 10% off the cover prices—quite a bargain! I understand that accepting the books and gift places me under no obligation ever to buy any books. I can always return a shipment and cancel at any time. Even if I never buy another book from Silhouette, the 4 free books and the surprise gift are mine to keep forever.

315 BPA A3UX

Name	(PLEASE PRINT)
Address	Apt. No.
City	Province Postal Code

This offer is limited to one order per household and not valid to present Silhouette Romance™ subscribers. *Terms and prices are subject to change without notice. Canadian residents will be charged applicable provincial taxes and GST.

CSROM-696   ©1990 Harlequin Enterprises Limited

The collection of the year!
NEW YORK TIMES BESTSELLING AUTHORS

Linda Lael Miller
Wild About Harry

Janet Dailey
Sweet Promise

Elizabeth Lowell
Reckless Love

Penny Jordan
Love's Choices

and featuring
Nora Roberts
The Calhoun Women

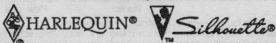
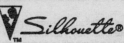

As seen on TV!
Free Gift Offer

With a Free Gift proof-of-purchase from any Silhouette® book,
you can receive a beautiful cubic zirconia pendant.

This gorgeous marquise-shaped stone is a genuine cubic
zirconia—accented by an 18" gold tone necklace.

(Approximate retail value $19.95)

Send for yours today...
compliments of ▼ *Silhouette*®
TM

To receive your free gift, a cubic zirconia pendant, send us one original proof-of-purchase, photocopies not accepted, from the back of any Silhouette Romance™, Silhouette Desire®, Silhouette Special Edition®, Silhouette Intimate Moments® or Silhouette Yours Truly™ title available in August, September or October at your favorite retail outlet, together with the Free Gift Certificate, plus a check or money order for $1.65 U.S./$2.15 CAN. (do not send cash) to cover postage and handling, payable to Silhouette Free Gift Offer. We will send you the specified gift. Allow 6 to 8 weeks for delivery. Offer good until October 31, 1996 or while quantities last. Offer valid in the U.S. and Canada only.

Free Gift Certificate

Name: _____

Address: _____

City: _____ State/Province: _____ Zip/Postal Code: _____

Mail this certificate, one proof-of-purchase and a check or money order for postage and handling to: SILHOUETTE FREE GIFT OFFER 1996. In the U.S.: 3010 Walden Avenue, P.O. Box 9077, Buffalo NY 14269-9077. In Canada: P.O. Box 613, Fort Erie, Ontario L2Z 5X3.

FREE GIFT OFFER   084-KMD
ONE PROOF-OF-PURCHASE
To collect your fabulous FREE GIFT, a cubic zirconia pendant, you must include this
original proof-of-purchase for each gift with the properly completed Free Gift Certificate.

084-KMD